TALES TO TELL

TALES
TO TELL

compiled by **David Campbell**

THE SAINT ANDREW PRESS · EDINBURGH ·

First published in 1986 by
THE SAINT ANDREW PRESS
121 George Street, Edinburgh

Copyright © 1986 The Saint Andrew Press

ISBN: 0 7152 0596 X

British Library Cataloguing in Publication Data
Tales to tell
  1. Bible stories, English
  I. Campbell, David
  220.9'505   BS551.2
  ISBN 0-7152-0596-X

*The Publisher acknowledges financial assistance from The
Drummond Trust towards the publication of this volume.*

Printed in Great Britain by
Holmes McDougall Ltd, Edinburgh, Scotland

CONTENTS

ACKNOWLEDGMENTS

The Publishers gratefully acknowledge and thank the following
individuals and schools for providing the illustrations, poems
and prayers which accompany the text in this book:

Georgie Goldie, Granton Primary School 9; Alan Robertson 12;
Knowetop Primary School 13; Albert Wills 15; Gary Mackinnon
17; Lesley Allan 19; Chris Cormack 24; Richard Begg 29; Scott
Marshall 31; Doreen 32; Jennifer, Arduthie Primary School 33;
Tracy King 34; Ann McKenzie 36; Penicuik and District Council
of Churches 37; Barbara, Prestonpans Primary School 38; Ross
McEwan 39; Eilidh Macdonald 41; Hazel Bonnella 43; Colin
McPhail 44; Louise Morrison 45; Kirsteen, Prestonpans Primary
School 49; Neil Hanning 50; Pamela, Prestonpans Primary School
52; Hazel, Prestonpans Primary School 57; James Wilson 59; Lynn
Chisholm 61; Louise, Prestonpans Primary School 63; Elise
Campbell 67; Karen Smith 68; Brian Sinclair 71; Mark Watson 77;
Pauline Archibald 79; Louise, Prestonpans Primary School 80; By
kind permission of the Iona Cathedral Trust 81; Lesley-Kay
Anderson 84 (above); Graham McGeoch 84 (below); Jonathan,
Prestonpans Primary School 85; Gregor Burns 86 (above); Adele
Birnie 86 (below); Lorna Dewar 87 (above); Julie Stephen 87
(below)

Cover illustrations by Paul Cooper, Lorna Dalgleish, Paula Willis
    and one unknown artist
Additional illustrations by William Keith Milne 47, 65, 69, 73
Cover and book design by William Ross
Adaptation of artwork by Lesley Ann Taylor

INTRODUCTION

These stories are for you to read to children. Childhood is a time to know and hear of beauty and courage and love, and from whom more appropriately than those closest: mums and dads and friends and teachers.

This is a book for children and adults to share in their age-old connection of story-telling. It is written with the conviction that it is not by listening to the voices of strangers on the media that power and beauty are best translated into the lives and imaginations of children, but by the immediate presence of people they know and love and trust.

The minds of children of this generation have been ubiquitously exposed to violence and the dark side of human nature and their own individual imaginations frequently stultified by the passive role of television addiction. The cult of media experts and stars, on the other hand, puts adults in danger of being brainwashed into the conviction that their own story-telling is inadequate. Nothing could be further from the truth.

This book has come about as a result of the popularity of stories in the BBC Scotland Education Department series, *A Scottish Religious Service for Primary Schools*:

'You have used modern versions of parables in your broadcasts. Are these published in a book?'

This and similar responses from teachers and their classes encouraged the BBC and The Saint Andrew Press to co-operate on just such a venture.

The classroom responses to the stories were very enthusiastic. For example, of Alan Spence's story, *Casual*:

'A fantastic story . . . terrific discussion . . . most successful.'

Of the modern version of *Esther*:

'Give us more Bible stories like the one we heard today!'

Some of the best stories from these broadcasts along with others commissioned from Scotland's leading writers form the contents of this book. Written to be read out to children between the ages of 7 and 11, they aim to be direct, simple and dramatic. The content is designed to appeal to both boys and girls and spans fantasy and reality, past and present, fact and fiction, football and fairy tales.

We hope that these stories kindle the individual imaginations of your children and plant seeds of inspiration, and, above all, that you enjoy this experience together.

DAVID CAMPBELL

𝒫ARABLES

THE FEAST IN THE CAVE

At first, no-one in the house really knew how Simon was spending all his pocket money and all his spare minutes. Not even his sister Katie, who was as bright as any eight year old could be and had the nose of a ferret after a rabbit for finding things out. And, of course, eventually Katie did find out, but for a while Simon would simply slip away mysteriously over the fence at the back of their garden into the woods, and vanish from the face of the earth somewhere near the old caravan that was always locked and that had once taken their mum and dad on holidays.

Katie asked Simon what he was up to.

'It's a secret,' said Simon.

'But who knows?' asked Katie.

'No-one knows or it wouldn't be a secret,' said Simon.

'Yes, but you know.'

'And that's why it's still a secret.'

'Tell me.'

'I might.'

'Well tell me something about your secret.'

'And who will you tell?'

'No-one.'

'No-one?'

'Nup, nope, no, not anybody living or dead, real or in books.' Katie had a rich imagination.

'Okay, I'll tell you,' Simon said finally. 'It's a place.'

'What sort of place?'

'A hiding place that no-one knows.'

'What's it like?'

'It's like a ship, and a palace and a cave and an aeroplane, and a temple and a grocer's shop, and the inside of a skull.'

Katie's eyes were wide. 'It can't be.'

'It is.' Simon's eyes were serious.

'Where is it?'

'Have you got the courage of a lion?'

'Yes.'

'Would you be afraid in the dark?'

'No.'

'Okay. I'll take you.'

'When?'

'Now.'

'But it isn't dark.'

'It will be. Do you really have the courage of a lion?'

'Yes. I'm ready.'

Simon pulled a long blue silk scarf out of his pocket, like a magician.

'What's that?'

'That is the dark.'

Katie laughed, snatched the scarf from Simon and began to wind it round and round her head and over her eyes.

'It's dark,' she said.

'Take my hand, little lion,' said Simon, and off they set. Katie had no idea where they were going, through the dark, on and on, but she stepped out as if it was broad daylight even though she could feel bushes brushing against her body like snakes.

'Now — piggyback!' Up she jumped.

'Now sit down here.' She sat down in the dark. She heard a creaking sound, a rattle.

'Walk up this slope. Stop. And now sit exactly here, on this throne. Wait.'

Katie waited. Another creak, a rattle, a click, a key turning in a lock. More clicks: click, click, click.

'Now. You can have eyes again,' said Simon, from somewhere above her head. Nimbly Katie unwound the blue silk scarf down to the last fold then blinked and blinked and blinked. She was surrounded by little lights of every colour in the rainbow: red and orange and yellow and green and blue and indigo and violet.

'It's not a ship, not a palace, it's not the inside of a skull . . . it's Aladdin's Cave,' she said.

'It's not Aladdin's Cave — it's the inside of a caravan.'

'And look at these magical lights.'

'They're not magical lights, they're coloured torches.'

'And you're floating on the ceiling.'

'I'm not floating on the ceiling, I'm lying on a bunk.'

'It's brilliant.'

'Yes, it's brilliant.' Simon laughed.

'How did you get in?'

Simon held up a big old key. 'Dad gave me this key.'

'What are you going to do here?'

'I'm going to have a feast.'
'Who are you going to invite?'
'My three best friends.'

Steven Fox was the cleverest boy in Primary 7. He had more computer games than anyone else in the school and he sometimes allowed Simon to play these games with him. His computer was the latest and best.

Hilda Smart was a dandelion clock of blonde curls; she was everyone's friend and had a flashing smile for every occasion. Simon thought secretly that she was lovely.

Jack Rush was neat as a pin and sharp as a knife. There was nothing he didn't know about football, and his father had once taken Simon and Jack in his Jaguar to a Premier League match between Celtic and Aberdeen.

'When, when are you going to have your feast?'
'On the seventh of July at three o'clock in the afternoon.'
'Can I help?'
'You can paint the most beautiful invitations in the world and deliver them by hand and bring back the replies. Invite them to a special place for an extra special surprise with extra-extra special food.'

Katie did this the very next day. She painted beautiful invitations on coloured paper and put them in silver envelopes and delivered them by hand. Steven and Hilda and Jack were all eager to come.

The inside of the secret caravan was crammed with everything you could think of from ten sorts of potato crisps to a huge chocolate birthday cake, and the decorations were magnificent. Three presents were hidden for the guests.

At three o'clock Simon and Katie were ready and waiting with an Aladdin's Cave full of surprises. Time passed. At four o'clock Katie went to see what had happened.

'They've all phoned up,' she said. 'Steven Fox can't come because he's trying out "Underworld", his new computer game; Hilda can't come because her new friend Clare is having a tea party and Jack Rush has got the chance to get the last sticker for his football album, so, well, anyway, he can't come either.'

For once Simon was angry. But he had an idea.
'Go out into the street,' he said, 'and invite the first three kids you meet, to come here at seven o'clock.'

Katie was delighted at this idea and skipped off, singing.

Dick Sneddon's dad was on the dole. Dick was as tough as a terrier, had one pair of worn-out shoes — but when he laughed it was like bursting a bag of confetti.

Harriet Wong's Chinese name meant Jade Beauty. She had been living in the street for two weeks and knew no-one, but she spoke English with a voice as clear as a river.

Red-haired Tom couldn't play games because of his lame leg and so was always the odd man out even though he had an imagination of fire.

These were the first three people that little Katie met. They were surprised and delighted and at seven o'clock exactly Simon opened the door and Katie led them into the secret feast in Simon's palace and ocean liner and spaceship and cave.

In the evening sunlight, high above the caravan, a beautiful many-coloured kite danced and curtsied in the sky. Below and beside the caravan, five laughing children with full stomachs chattered and planned while they watched the technicolour fish swimming above them in the air. Harriet had shown them how to make a Chinese Kite.

And from Simon — Tom, Dick and Harriet took home from the caravan the three secret presents that had been meant for Steven, Jack and Hilda.

Biblical reference: Luke 14:15–24   ∎

What is a friend?

A friend is very special,
He'll help you when you're bad,
He'll play with you when you are bored,
and tell jokes when you're sad.

My Friend came round last Friday,
His Christian name is Steve,
We had a disagreement,
So I asked him to leave.

But because a friend is special,
I asked for us to meet,
He thought about it carefully,
He's coming round next week.

A Friend

A friend is someone who
cares all the time,
A friend is someone who wont
snap "Thats mine",
A friend will play with you day
after day,
A friend wont call you lots
of names, instead she'll
invent lots of games.

A FRIEND

CASUAL

Jimmy knew there was going to be trouble when he heard the noise out in the street. He lived near Ibrox stadium and the crowds passed right by his close on their way from the game. Rangers had been playing Aberdeen, and all afternoon he had listened to the roars. He had realised something was wrong when he'd looked out of his window and seen a steady stream of Rangers supporters leaving early.

He'd gone through to the living room where his father was watching *Grandstand*. Jimmy found it really boring — snooker, wrestling, boxing, darts. Football was the only sport that interested him at all. He played for his school team. He wanted to be a great winger like Davie Cooper. But his father wouldn't take him to the games any more, because of all the bother.

His mother was in the kitchen, making the tea. The final scores came up on the teleprinter, and sure enough Rangers had lost.

Then the noise in the street began to get really loud. Usually the police would manage to keep the two sets of supporters apart. But right out there, outside Jimmy's window, was where the two streams met. And that's where there was *always* trouble.

The first thing he heard was the chanting — the victors' triumphant singsong.

'Aberdeen! Aberdeen! Aberdeen!'

Then from the opposite direction came a great angry roaring, trying to shout the other lot down.

'Rangers! Rangers!'

He could hear the two sides getting closer and closer, the noise getting louder and louder, till they clashed head-on.

Jimmy's father tore himself away from the TV to come and look. And even his mother came through from the kitchen. It was terrible to watch. It wasn't just a fist-fight. They went in with the head, with the boot, with sticks, bottles, anything they could lay their hands on. Then the police waded in and somehow they managed to break it up, drive a wedge between the two sides. They arrested quite a few — bundled them into black Marias. Then they formed a cordon round a squad of Aberdeen supporters, and they marched them off down the road into the town centre.

'Probably escort them right into the station and onto the train,' said Jimmy's father. 'And good riddance!'

He closed the curtains and sat down again in front of the TV.

'It used to be just Rangers and Celtic supporters,' he said. 'But now Aberdeen are up there at the top of the heap, and that's changed everything. I'm telling you, I've seen fights in my time, outside that window, but I don't think I've ever seen anything like today. Mind you, they were just saying on the telly there, the game itself was a bit of a bloodbath. Two players sent off. Bookings on both sides. It's no wonder the violence flares up on the terracing. I mean what do they expect?'

'I don't know,' said his mother, setting down plates on the table. 'I really don't.'

'Do you know what gets me?' said his father. 'Most of these troublemakers are young. I mean they're just boys. What is it they call themselves? "Casuals." I was reading about it. All the big clubs attract them now — Liverpool and the rest. And half of them aren't even all that interested in the football. They just come along to cause bother.'

'Terrible,' said his mother.

'It wasn't like that when I was a boy,' went on his father. 'And that's not so long ago really. My father could take me to the match without having to worry about being beaten up just for wearing the wrong colours.'

He looked at Jimmy.

'I wouldn't take you at all. Wouldn't risk it.'

Jimmy squirmed, feeling miserable. 'I know' he said.

'That carry-on in Brussels was the last straw,' said his father. 'The riots and everything. Turned my stomach so it did.'

'What's it got to do with sport?' said his mother. 'That's what I want to know.'

'Of course it's not just football,' said his father. 'It's everywhere you turn. They say it's because there's too much violence on TV. But I don't know.'

'What's on tonight?' asked his mother.

'Och the usual rubbish. Wogan. Noel Edmonds. Still, it passes the time.'

When he'd finished his tea, Jimmy went back through to his room. There was nothing he wanted to see on TV till *Sportscene* later on. His father usually let him stay up and watch it. He read through his football annuals. Then he took his coloured pens and tried to copy a picture of Davie Cooper, to put up on his wall.

He didn't know how long he'd been sitting there when he heard the commotion outside. It sounded like a scuffle — a lot of yelling, then footsteps, like two or three people running away. He pulled open the curtains, just enough to peer out. At first he couldn't see anything. The street looked deserted, nobody in sight. Then he saw him, slumped in the doorway of the shop across the road. He couldn't make out the man's face, but he could see the red and white scarf. An Aberdeen supporter. Jimmy watched for a minute or two, expecting the man to pick himself up

and go staggering off down the road. But he didn't move.

Jimmy ran through to the living room.

'There's a man out there! He's been hurt!'

His parents came over to the window.

'Probably drunk,' said his mother.

'Paralytic,' said his father.

'No!' said Jimmy. 'I think some people beat him up and ran away. I heard them.'

'Well,' said his mother, 'the police'll come along and find him. Or somebody'll report it.'

'Right,' said his father, closing the curtains. 'Anyway he was probably asking for it. Probably one of these casuals, causing bother.'

Wogan was interviewing some woman, a film star. He spoke to her face on a giant video screen.

Jimmy went back through to his room. He tried to read his book again, finish his drawing. But his heart wasn't in it. He kept thinking about the man lying out there. What if he was dying?

He went to the window again and looked out. The figure was still sprawled in the doorway, not moving.

A young couple came by and the boy went to have a look. But the girl pulled him away, arguing.

The next one to pass was a drunk, unsteady on his feet. He stopped, and stared. Jimmy heard his voice, very loud.

'Ach aye,' he said, 'there's always somebody worse off than yourself.' And off he went, reeling down the road.

Jimmy went back through to the living room.

Wogan was still interviewing the giant face. He had made some joke and the screen was filled with an enormous grin. Jimmy's father started channel-popping. He had a remote-control gadget so he could flick from channel to channel without having to get up out of his seat. Wogan gave way to a car chase, and a quiz show, and a news report on famine in Africa.

'Terrible thing that,' said his mother. 'Doesn't anybody care?'

Again Jimmy went to his own room, and looked out. There was still no sign of life. Cars passed by. Nobody stopped. A few more people passed by on foot. One man went over to have a look. The rest crossed over to the other side of the street. Jimmy felt he had to say something to his parents. He stuck his head round the door.

'That man's still lying there.'

'Listen son,' said his father, 'we don't want to get involved. I mean we could end up getting called to court as witnesses. No point in saying you didn't see anything.'

'And then where are you?' said his mother. 'Your name's in the paper.'

'You end up getting your windows put in,' said his father. 'No thanks!'

'Well couldn't you just *phone* the police?' said Jimmy.

'Same thing would happen,' said his mother. 'They'd ask for our name and address.'

'Just forget it son,' said his father. 'And stay away from the window.'

But he couldn't forget it. He sat on his bed thinking about the man, wishing there was something he could do. Then he heard the voice, out in the street and coming closer, singing over and over.

> 'Oh Oh Oh Rangers! Rangers!
> I'd walk a million miles
> For one of your goals
> Oh Rangers!'

Jimmy looked out and saw him on the other side of the road — a boy about 17 in a Rangers scarf. He saw the figure in the doorway and he stopped and moved towards it.

Jimmy was scared now. He was sure the boy was going to murder the Aberdeen supporter, finish him off. He wanted to shout out but his father had told him not to get involved, to stay away from the window. He didn't know what to do.

The boy bent over the Aberdeen supporter and had a close look. Then he helped him up to a sitting position.

'Hey, pal,' he said. 'You're in some state!'

The boy ran to the phone-box at the next corner. But it wasn't working. It was always vandalised.

Then he tried to flag down a passing car, but nobody would stop.

Then he saw Jimmy, at the window. He stared straight at him. Then he pointed to the man in the doorway and mimed making a phone call. Jimmy nodded and beckoned. The boy started across the road.

Jimmy went through and told his parents. 'There's a boy coming across, to phone.'

'Eh?' said his father.

'What have you been up to?' asked his mother.

'I told you to stay away from that window!'

'See *you*!'

The doorbell rang.

His mother turned off the TV. 'We could just not answer it,' she whispered.

'Ach what's the use?' said his father. 'He's seen Jimmy.'

He opened the door and the boy in the Rangers scarf stood there.

'There's a guy out there in a bad way,' he said. 'Can I use your phone?'

'Sure.'

The boy phoned quickly.

'Thanks,' he said.

'Not at all,' said Jimmy's father.

The boy went back across the road and the three of them watched again from the window. The man in the doorway seemed to be shivering. The boy took off his jacket and put it round him. When the ambulance arrived it was followed by a police car. The boy watched the injured man being carefully lifted on a stretcher. One of the ambulancemen gave him back his jacket. Then they drove off, with the lights flashing and the siren wailing.

'I suppose we did the right thing,' said Jimmy's father.

'I suppose so,' said his mother.

The boy waved across to Jimmy, gave him the thumbs up. Jimmy waved back.

Biblical reference: Luke 10:30–37   ■

Dear Lord
give us the power to help other people when they are in need of help and think of other people before yourself. Help other people who are starving in the wide world, and make their crops grow
Amen

A GIFT FOR THE PRINCESS

It was a dreich winter day nearing the end of January. For the whole of the long dark month in the ancient Kingdom of Calandia fierce winds had blown, blizzards of snow had covered the land and the sky was dark as night. The sun with a cold white eye made a dim circle around the horizon each day before returning once more into another long night's sleep. It seemed like an eternal winter, but in the stone castle everyone was busy making last minute preparations. While the wind had whistled and raged outside the castle, inside had been a-bustle for the whole long month. For the second last day of January was to be a celebration. The Prince Torquil was to be engaged to Princess Savourna of the neighbouring Kingdom of Edonia.

Everyone from the highest lords of the land to the poorest people was excited and glad because the match seemed to be so perfect. The Prince was as handsome as she was beautiful and both of them were the darlings of their nations' hearts.

Because the celebration was so very special, the King of Calandia, Ranald Redbeard, had created a giant competition. All of his subjects were invited to offer an entertainment for the royal couple. Whoever had an idea was to take it to the house of the Royal Master of Entertainments, knock on the door and tell him. If he liked the idea they were to be allowed through the door to tell the King himself. For this reason the King called his competition 'Opportunity Knocks' and was very proud of the title.

Of course all manner of people came with their special entertainments — jugglers, fire swallowers, clowns, acrobats — and many brought beautiful ornaments carved from wood, and garments they had fashioned out of wool or leather or silk. But the King frowned. 'I've seen all of this stuff before: jugglers juggling, fire swallowers fire swallowing, clowns clowning, acrobats acrobatting. No, this is not good enough for such an engagement. I want, I need, I demand something special!'

Now three friends were meeting in a little wooden hut outside the castle. They were the gypsy Mirelda who had eyes of coal and feet that danced like flickering flames, the tinker Seannachie whose tongue lilted with stories that would open the eyes of the blind with wonder, and the minstrel Lutan who made songs that could create rivers of tears or waterfalls of laughter. And he could play the fiddle like an angel or a devil. They had a special and a secret plan. They were going to take from their imaginations the greatest treasures they had, and from their hearts the sweetest words, and make their gift to the Princess and the Prince the loveliest and best story that had ever been told; and they were going to tell it with the silver words of Seannachie's tongue, the golden flames of Mirelda's dancing feet and the glowing rubies of Lutan's song and the diamonds of his magic fiddle. It was a story made with love and when they rehearsed it even the robins in the cold snow flew from bare branch to bare branch in delight as if they could hear the voice of summer.

One other person too was busy making his own preparations. It was Bron, the court magician. He had been mysteriously busy, was heard muttering spells, had a glint like electrical sparks in his eyes, and was building a huge frame out of a metal that only he knew the secret of. It was going to be a powerful magic. Strange sounds not unlike the voices of humans could be heard coming from his laboratory workshop, strange notes not unlike the music of a fiddle and a noise something like a song. Everyone was filled with curiosity but the secret was locked in his silent and thoughtful frown.

The day and the hour came when the King was to make his decision. The redbreasted robins had carried rumours of the wonderful story of Lutan and Mirelda and Seannachie, and the walls of the castle itself trembled with whispers of Bron's secret invention. What would the King decide? What was Bron's wonderful invention? The Royal approval was to be for one or the other.

Into the great hall, before the King and his son Torquil, came Lutan and Mirelda and Seannachie and told their story with music and words and dancing; the Prince watched as if he saw a bright dream and his heart flew with joy like a robin redbreast in the snow. Bron watched motionlessly. Then he leaned towards the King and whispered in his ear. The King's eyes opened wide with

A Grace for a Wedding.

We thankyou Lord for what we have,
For what we get,
We thankyou Lord for this special day,
We thankyou for this wedding,
You gave us churches, ministers and us,
We need them for the wedding.
Amen.

astonishment and then he nodded his head and gripped Bron by the arm and smiled. He raised his hand and stopped the entertainment.

'I have decided,' he said.

The Prince's dark eyes were puzzled and troubled.

'But father,' he said, 'what can Bron possibly have that is lovelier than this gypsy story?'

'Nothing I'm sure, my young Prince.'

'But then why?'

'No more questions. You will see a miracle.'

And so it was that Redbeard stood with shining eyes on the balcony to make his announcement. The Prince sat beside him in a winter of gloom.

'My people of Calandia,' said the King, 'I have sought far and wide to find an entertainment worthy enough to welcome the Princess Savourna from Edonia and to celebrate her engagement to my son, Torquil. At last I have found something that is really new. It is a work of genius that will bring honour to our Kingdom and be a fitting entertainment for the royal couple.

At that moment three figures could be seen departing from a side door and melting quietly into the crowd. If you had looked closely you would have seen that the feet of Mirelda the Gypsy trod leadenly, that Seannachie's silver tongue was silent, and the minstrel for once had no song, but they joined bravely in the clapping when the King said:

'And so the entertainment from Bron's Magic Story Maker will begin, not during the day but at midnight before the last day of January.'

Everyone clapped and went home full of curiosity. What was this invention, whoever had heard of a magic story maker and, above all, why should the celebration be at midnight when it was the very dead of winter?

Now, the Princess Savourna had been brought up in the Kingdom of Edonia in very simple ways. Her favourite colours were yellow and white, the colours of daisies and dandelions and these were, even for a Princess, her favourite flowers. When she was little she had loved nothing so much as to dance in the green fields amongst wild flowers. The gypsy people had told her wonderful country names for dandelions that made her laugh when she was sad and gave her courage when she was afraid: funny names like Bum Pipe, Burning Fire, Lion's Teeth, Piss-a-bed, and lovely names like Clock Flower and Wishes.

The Princess Savourna though had always carried one darkness around with her like a shadow. When she was no higher than a man's waist, the gypsy people had left and with them the brown boy who was the warmest and deepest friend of her childhood. And she didn't even know his name. Without word or warning in the night the whole gypsy encampment with their stories and songs and violins and dances and mystical fires had disappeared from her life.

But now that she was to marry the Prince Torquil, perhaps the shadow would leave her.

The great day came. And as the pink sun slipped out of sleep into the dark blue sky, Princess Savourna rode in her golden carriage, drawn by four white mares out of the Kingdom of Edonia, towards her meeting with the Prince.

A long journey it was. Out of night and into day and back towards the dark. When the disc of the sun was half of a yellow penny against the mountain, the Princess arrived. In a bed of thistle and dandelion down, she slept all through the day in the castle.

She rose, full of sunshine, like a field of dandelions and daisies, laughing and smiling. Then her dainty ladies-in-waiting told her she was not to meet her Prince until midnight when the King was to announce their engagement to all the people of the land. Bron, the court magician, was to offer an entertainment so new that it would astonish the whole world more than a mushroom. Midnight seemed a long time away.

Patiently she waited through the thin winter day. At last the dusky sun fell out of the sky and a curved moon rose towards midnight in the dark blue sky.

Suddenly she was afraid, as if once again her gypsy boy and the smoking tents of his gypsy people had left her and she was alone again. All alone.

In red and in gold, the court chamberlain near midnight came to fetch her to the celebration and meeting with her Prince. But it was strange. It was night. It was dark, and clouds hung over the moon. It was black as the horses that now drew her carriage. She was hurried through the shadows and heard occasional whispers like the wind through bushes.

The carriage stopped and she stepped out into the cold night air. The coachman took her and led her to a throne, where she sat alone and as cold as stone. He told her the Prince was by her side on his throne but she could not see or touch him. She felt the crowd of silent people gathered in the dark and, like her, they were waiting and frightened although they did not say so. At long last, a voice, the voice of the King, burst through the blackness.

'My people of Calandia — now we celebrate.' He said nothing else.

The voice of Bron the magician forked like an electrical current into the air. 'High Majesty, Prince Torquil and Princess Savourna, people of Calandia, I offer you the greatest invention of all the ages for your entertainment. You need do nothing but sit; it will do everything else — everything. It does not need people to help or even join in. I call it the Distant Picture Maker; it is a magic story-teller. Now watch.'

Like dark falling, silence descended on the huge crowd. Before them rose at first a strange unearthly light, a white glow. And then it seemed to become a huge square metal frame shimmering like molten lead. Above their heads it rose like a giant window frame filled with an eerie pale light; and then the miracle. Dimly at first but surely, yes, strange shapes like the figures of people began to appear, and a noise like fiddle music arose, and a sound, very like a human voice, and the figures began to flicker and move. The crowd stirred uneasily. And now unbelievably the figures in the giant picture became like the ghosts of Mirelda and Seannachie and Lutan — but how could that be, for Lutan and Seannachie and Mirelda stood here in the silenced crowd, watching. The people were amazed, mesmerised like rabbits before the swaying head of a rattlesnake. And their children were as still as stone, not squirming and giggling and playing like children at all, but silent statues with their eyes fixed on this wonder before them.

The eyes of Bron the court magician burned with pride. And now the giant frame was completely filled with a huge picture of Seannachie's head as if it had no body, and his mouth boomed out a story in a voice very like his own.

Suddenly a child's cry cut the night air in a wild scream of fear. 'Seannachie, Seannachie, stop, stop, I am afraid.'

But still the giant head talked on as if deaf and blind and untouchable. As if nothing anyone said or did could ever stop it, as if it did not care what people thought or felt, even if children were howling in terror. A tremble ran through the crowd. The knife edge of the moon slid into the sea and in the first faint pink of the sun a huge tear could be seen to run down the pale cheek of the Princess Savourna.

It was then in the first light that the Prince saw Savourna and the tear glistening like a dew drop on her face. She looked so fragile and alone. He rose from his throne and came to her.

'What is the matter, Savourna?' he asked gently. She turned from the giant picture and saw him. For the first time that she had been in the Kingdom of Calandia, she smiled. And it was as if she had switched on the sun. Everywhere seemed brighter in the light of her smile.

She looked into Torquil's eyes and said:

'What is the matter? Everything was the matter until now.' He held her hand. 'But now I feel welcome at last.'

Just then the King appeared.

'What is this?' he demanded. 'The entertainment is not yet over.'

Savourna turned to the large King. She seemed very small beside him and she said, 'I do not like this entertainment. I do not like its gleaming eye. It is like being in a prison and alone. These figures are not real. They do not listen or see. It is no welcome at all to be welcomed by pictures. Once I knew real gypsies with camp fires and real dances and songs and stories and everything.'

Like lightning, then thunder, there was a huge flash and a great echoing crash. Seannachie, the real story-teller, had thrown a rock at his face in the midst of the huge metal frame. Like a volcano erupting there were flames and rumbles and smoke and dust, and as the smoky vapour cleared, Bron's great machine was no more. It had vanished.

The silence was like the silence at the very beginning of the world. The Prince whispered something in his father's ear. Redbeard did something very unusual for him. He smiled and said:

'Seannachie, Mirelda and Lutan, come here, now.'

The three made their way through the crowd.

'My son wishes to say something.'

'My gypsy friends,' said Torquil, 'we would like you to welcome the Princess Savourna with your living story of dances and songs.'

'What a lovely welcome,' said Savourna, delighted. 'What a beautiful present.'

And when Savourna saw the three gypsies, she exclaimed aloud, 'Do you know this is a miracle, Torquil?'

'No,' said Torquil. 'What do you mean?'

'Why these are my very own gypsies!' she told him. 'Yes, I played with them when I was a child and I lost them. And here they are now to welcome me.'

'They will always welcome you,' said Torquil. 'You know they gave me a present to give you.'

'What is it?' asked Savourna.

Torquil whispered in her ear and she burst into petals of laughter and he pressed into her hand a flower. It was a dandelion. She threw a daisy chain around his neck and kissed him gently.

■

THE DAY DUNCAN CAME BACK

Duncan Miller was fed up. He'd never been so low in his life. His whole world seemed to be falling apart and here was another wet Saturday. He looked through the rain on the window. It was like tears flowing down. If he hadn't mucked everything up he could be playing football for his school team. But he'd blown it and it was all his fault.

Yes, you had to admit it, Duncan Miller was a good footballer. He scored lots of goals. He worked hard with his team mates and in fact he was one of the most popular players around.

'That player will go places,' said Mr Stephen, the school gym teacher. 'If he sticks in, he could make a career out of football. Best player we've ever had in the school team.'

Duncan's own hero was Kenny Dalglish, although with his bright red hair and his ability to grab opportunities like a ferret he looked more like Gordon Strachan. But anyhow the team couldn't have been playing better. Duncan was the ideal striker and his feed was nearly always Andy McDonald, dark-haired, cool, and able to lay a pass at your feet as neatly as a dart in the double sixteen.

That year Duncan broke the school record for the number of goals scored in a season. At that time playing for the school team was all Duncan hoped for. Then came the big game with Dunbreck School, always a tough one. The score stood at one-all and the village clock said the referee's whistle should go at any second, when Andy McDonald took a ball from the feet of a Dunbreck player and sent a high cross towards Duncan. Two players were covering him but somehow he headed the ball between them and hit the sweetest first-timer you've ever seen, swinging past the Dunbreck goalie and crunching into the net. A stunner. But that was the last ball Duncan kicked for his school team. A new youth club team had started up and their manager, George Geech, got hold of Duncan.

'Look son, we're going places, we're looking for the cream. Don't waste any more time, head for the big time with us.'

That Monday morning at the interval, Duncan sought out Mr Stephen.

'Can I see you for a minute, sir?' asked Duncan.

'Yes laddie, what is it you want?'

'Well, sir, it's like this. I don't think I'll be able to play on Saturday, sir.'

'Can't play? Goodness laddie, are you sick? What's the matter?'

'Well, sir, I think I've done all I can with this team. There's a new team starting in the youth club in the village and they play Saturday mornings too. And they've asked me to play for them sir. And I'd like to go, sir. So I won't be able to play for the school any more.'

Duncan waited for the explosion but there wasn't one. He'd been sure Mr Stephen would rage at him and try to stop him going. But he didn't. He just shrugged his shoulders and said, 'Aye well, laddie. I cannae hold you back. If you want to go, who am I to stop you? I've taught you all I can. Off you go, and play for your youth club.'

Duncan was delighted. 'Great,' he thought. 'Here's my big chance. I'll make a name for myself in the youth club. And then, who knows — maybe Scotland!' His imagination danced. He'd be a success. And for a while that's just how it was.

George Geech was a shrewd manager: he could spot good players and he poached them unscrupulously from other young teams in the neighbourhood. He caused a lot of ill-feeling locally but he put together a smooth football team.

Duncan had never felt better. He scored goals as if it was a habit, and he was everyone's hero. They would jump on him, pat his back, and one day they even carried him off the pitch, shoulder high, when he'd scored the winning goal. Things couldn't have been better. The only trouble was George Geech's ambition. The players had to contribute their pocket money — 'It's for publicity, lads, fares to see good players, for the future. We've got to think ahead.'

Then there was the jealousy in the youth club team. Two of the players resented Duncan's popularity. That was bad enough off the pitch but it began to happen in games. Duncan in one game was unmarked with a clear shot at goal but he didn't get the ball and the team began to lose. They fought amongst themselves, blamed each other and had a string of defeats. Then the last blow fell. Duncan was dropped and told his job was to look after the boots and keep his eye on the kit. His world fell apart and two more weeks passed. No game for Duncan. Then he heard the news that George Geech, the manager of the youth club team, had disappeared. That would have been good news but he took all the club funds with him and the youth club team was disbanded.

And so sitting miserably at home on this wet Saturday morning Duncan broke down sobbing miserably and was thinking to himself, 'It's all gone wrong. I don't even have any friends left. I wish I'd never left the school team.'

And there and then, Duncan made a decision. He'd go back and tell Mr Stephen he wanted to be back with the school team again. He wouldn't even ask to play. He'd be quite happy to clean the boots or fix the nets or carry the strips. All he wanted was to be back where he belonged. *That's* what he'd do. He'd go back where he began.

Duncan's school team were playing at home. Mr Stephen was not in a good mood.

'It's pathetic,' he moaned in the dressing room. 'Here we are with an important game and we don't have a single substitute. No-one's bothered to turn up. Afraid of a bit of rain I suppose. If anyone gets injured we'll only have ten men.'

And the game didn't cheer him up either. It was wet, blustery and cold and the game seemed as drab as the weather. By sheer determination the team managed to get to the end of the first half with no goals scored on any side.

'Aye, well, keep it up, lads,' he said at half time, 'and at all costs keep out of trouble!'

Two minutes into the second half disaster struck. Andy McDonald, playing his usual committed game, went into a hard tackle and came off limping badly. 'No use, sir, I can't go on.'

Mr Stephen nodded. 'Well that's it,' he thought, 'down to ten men, against a crack team. No chance.'

Then, in the distance, coming into the school playing fields he noticed a small boy.

'Who on earth is coming to watch the game in *this*

weather,' muttered Mr Stephen. And then as the figure approached, Mr Stephen recognised him as Duncan Miller.

'Duncan,' he said, 'what on earth are you doing here?'

'Well, sir, things didn't work out too well with the youth club team. I know I shouldn't have come back sir, but I just wanted to say I was sorry. Can I stay with the team, sir? I'll clean the boots sir, anything sir. Please can I stay, sir?'

For the first time that wet Saturday the clouds left Mr Stephen's craggy brow and his face broke into a big smile. Suddenly it stopped raining as if to celebrate.

'Ach, don't be daft laddie. Clean the boots!' He laughed. 'Get yourself changed, as quick as you like. Oh, and Andy, bring Duncan your shirt. Get him a pair of boots. And hurry, laddie, we've got our player back.'

The school team didn't win that day but they kept the crack opposition to a draw. The dressing room buzzed and crackled with excitement. Suddenly the door burst open. Mr Stephen came in staggering under a huge load.

'Hot pies, boys — crisps, squash and, for anyone who wants it, ice-cream! We're going to celebrate Duncan's return.'

There were cheers and backslapping and laughing: it was like a party. Everyone tucked in and the cold outside was forgotten.

In one corner, alone, Andy McDonald sat glowering.

'What's up, Andy?' asked Mr Stephen.

'Well, it just doesn't seem fair, sir!'

'What doesn't?'

'Well, sir, we've been here every Saturday and we've worked hard for the team for weeks. Why such a fuss about Duncan? He hasn't even been around. He was even playing for another team till it went bust.'

'Aye, well, son,' began Mr Stephen, 'it is a bit strange maybe but I rely on you, Andy, and you're the team backbone, but I thought Duncan was gone for good, that we'd lost him, and it's just great that we found him again. See what I mean, son?'

But Andy still looked puzzled.

Biblical reference: Luke 15: 11-32 ∎

A CHRISTMAS PARABLE

The night was cold and dark. The ground had a white coat of snow and in the sky was a slice of yellow moon with one bright star by her side. The street lamps had haloes, the street was empty. One by one windows were blacked out as curtains were drawn, shutting out the cold, shutting out the dark, shutting out the world. Inside the houses, people were going about their business unaware that a lone figure of a young woman was approaching: Beatrice pulled her worn blue jacket more closely about her body to keep out the wind. She had been walking now for hours, searching for shelter, searching for a place to take the precious gift she was carrying. Surely she was near her journey's end? Surely she was near the place she was looking for. As she glanced along the dismal street she realised that she did not know for certain which door would open to welcome her, nor who was to receive the precious gift. What she did know was that she must find shelter for the night.

Taking a deep breath, Beatrice straightened her jacket and tried to smooth her hair. She must look a bit scruffy, she hadn't had time over the past few days to wash or tidy herself up properly; she'd been too concerned with finding somewhere to live for a while . . . and then there was the gift to consider.

The door she stopped at was a wooden one with lots of little windows in it. Beatrice could see movement inside, and she was a bit nervous. Was this the right place? She knocked on the door.

Inside the house, things were hectic. Gordon and Alexis Campbell were preparing for a Christmas party.

'Alexis, have you seen that silver wrapping paper? The stuff on a roll, you know; I left it on the sideboard.'

'For goodness' sake don't bother me — can't you see I'm busy? Use something else, it doesn't matter what you use, they're only going to rip it up anyway. Let me see . . . I've invited the Martins; did you speak to Bill Craig at the office? Oh, I'd better send an invitation anyway — people never feel really invited unless they get something in writing. What do you think about the mince pies — have I made enough? Come on Gordon, stop dithering, there's lots to do.'

'Was that the door, Alexis?'

'What? I didn't hear anything. Well, what about the mince pies, what do you think?'

'It *was* the door,' Gordon was sure.

'Well answer it then — who on earth could it be at this time? Just what I need, as if I haven't got enough to do without having visitors to cope with too. I'll just finish this list then I'll see to the turkey. Answer the door!'

Fixing a pleasant welcome on his face, Gordon Campbell opened the door. His welcome fell when he saw the bedraggled girl standing on his doorstep. She was dressed all in blue, but everything looked old; her hair was scraped from her face and crammed into a rather odd-looking beret.

Beatrice stared over Gordon Campbell's shoulder and into the warm bright kitchen. There were piles of presents, some wrapped, some not, lying casually on the table and sideboard. There was coloured paper everywhere; cards and decorations; tinsel and flickering fairy lights. Alexis

Sharing

On Christmas day I shared my presents with all of my family except my gran who was in Australia. Every body in my family wanted something. My mum wanted to read my Rupert book (50th Anniversary), my dad wanted to see my mouse candle and my brother wanted to see my football, my BMX gear and more. God made us share by his skill and power. Some of my friends came down and brought one of their presents and we shared our presents together. That evening we all shared our sweets, rock, lollipops and other things.

Campbell was sitting at a table clack-clack-clacking away at a typewriter; faster and faster her hands moved on the keys in a frantic attempt to keep up with her yakking tongue as she kept up a constant commentary on what she had done, what she was doing, and what she was going to do.

'Yes?' said Gordon impatiently to the waif-like figure before him. 'Are you looking for someone?'

Beatrice wasn't sure if this was the place. She spoke hesitantly.

'I'm looking for somewhere to stay . . . I've got something special . . . a gift.'

'Who is that, Gordon?' came Alexis' shrill voice (the typewriter didn't even miss a clack). 'Gordon — hurry up, I need you to address these invitation cards.'

Gordon glanced back at his wife and knew she wouldn't welcome this interruption, especially when she saw who was doing the interrupting. He wasn't too pleased himself, come to that — he had lots to do, it was Christmas after all: a busy time. This was holding him back. He decided in that instant to get rid of this scruffy girl and get on with his Christmas preparations.

'Well I'm sorry dear, but you can't stay here. We've no room. We're rather busy, as you can see, and I really don't have time to stand here chatting.'

Beatrice wasn't going to be put off that easily. She *had* to find somewhere to stay, time was marching on.

'If I could just come in for a minute.'

At this point, Alexis stopped typing. 'What on earth's going on, Gordon,' she demanded. 'And who is *that*?' she added, looking in horror at Beatrice. Gordon shrugged apologetically, but Alexis was having none of it.

'Get out, you tyke!' she snapped, and slammed the door. 'Honestly Gordon, you should have more sense, standing on the doorstep chatting when you know we've got so much to do — look — that's the mince pies ready: take them out of the oven would you, there's a dear . . . I've almost finished the invitations.'

Beatrice turned away and walked on down the street. The next house was set well back from the road — a large house with a gravel driveway leading to a holly and ivy wreathed front door. Beatrice trudged up the path, paused for a moment and knocked on the door. Behind the door the atmosphere was heavy with perfume and cigar smoke — Douglas and Jennifer Hamilton-Armstrong were entertaining some friends.

'. . . And so I told them not to be so ridiculous, but simply to charge it to my account. Another drink, old chap? Jen, my sweet, would you fetch another brandy for Charles here while I circulate a bit?'

'Answer the door, Douglas, that'll be the Hendersons.' Douglas Hamilton-Armstrong threw open the door in an expansive gesture and smiled charitably down at the girl in blue on the doorstep. Beatrice didn't speak.

'Well, my dear,' asked Douglas Hamilton-Armstrong, 'can I do something for you?'

'The question is,' said Beatrice quietly, 'can I do something for you?'

'How amusing. What can you possibly do for us — you'd better come in and join our little party. Look everyone, we've got an unexpected guest who wants to do something for us — fetch her a drink, somebody.'

'No thank you,' said Beatrice. All eyes were now on her.

'Is she a gypsy?' asked someone. 'Perhaps she'll tell our fortunes!' A wave of laughter rippled round the room.

'I'm not a gypsy,' Beatrice said, 'but I do have a special gift.'

'Oh goody — a guessing game! No — don't tell us what it is, let us guess. . . .' Giggles.

'You don't have any parcels, it must be something small — is it in your pocket?'

'No,' said Beatrice, 'it is not.'

'Is it valuable?'

'What could she have of any value?'

Beatrice looked around the room. 'My gift is so precious you could not, with all your wealth, buy it. But I will give you it if you offer me what I need.'

'What do you need? Food? Come on then, there's lots to eat; here, have a little smoked salmon. No? What about some Christmas pud, then? Would you like something to drink? Brandy? Champagne?'

'Come on then, what's this precious gift of yours — let's see it.'

'It's something you've always wanted but don't already have,' said Beatrice.

'Well it can't be brandy, then,' hiccupped Charles, 'we've plenty of that!'

'It can't be jewels,' said a rather tall woman, clanking with bracelets.

'It certainly isn't food,' said Jennifer Hamilton-Armstrong, crisply. 'I made certain we wouldn't be short of that.'

'It isn't money,' said Douglas Hamilton-Armstrong, taking a fat wallet from his inside pocket. 'Come along dear, tell us what you want from us and then you can run along.' He was beginning to tire of the game.

'I need somewhere to stay.'

'Oh.' A pause. 'I see. Well, this isn't a hotel you know — and as you can see we have rather a full house tonight. Look — you take this.' He tried to press a ten pound note into Beatrice's hand. 'And I'm sure that'll buy you a bed for the night.' Douglas Hamilton-Armstrong began to lead Beatrice to the door.

'I don't want your money,' Beatrice said. 'That's not what I need.'

Douglas Hamilton-Armstrong was rather irritated by this scruffy girl's attitude — what was she playing at, hadn't they offered her enough? He opened the door.

'Well in that case,' he said smartly, 'get out, you are wasting our time!' Pushing Beatrice out, he slammed the door behind her. This action was accompanied by gales of laughter from the party guests, and they turned back to their merry-making. It was as if Beatrice had never been there at all.

After the heat of the big house, the night felt colder than ever. Beatrice hoped she wouldn't have to search for very much longer; her feet were aching and she was tired. But she knew that the Hamilton-Armstrongs hadn't been ready to receive her gift — their house hadn't been the right house.

The cottage she came to next looked ordinary enough — perhaps this was the place she'd been looking for.

Beatrice walked up to the door and knocked loudly.

'I'll get the door, Hugh. Turn the TV down for a minute, it's awful loud.' Alice MacIntosh and her husband Hugh had been sitting by the fire enjoying a quiet evening on their own before the hubbub of the Christmas festivities caught up with them. She was taken aback when she saw Beatrice, and wasn't going to invite her in at first, but when she heard about Beatrice's plight she thought it was her duty to do something for this poor soul, so obviously tired and shivering from the cold. Anyway, it wouldn't do for the neighbours to see Beatrice standing on the doorstep: what would they think if she turned her away into the cold?

'You'd better come away in then,' offered Alice, just as Hugh came through to see what was keeping her.

'So you've nowhere to stay?' asked Hugh, after he'd been told. 'Well, I'll put the kettle on for some tea while we decide what to do for the best.'

'Never mind the kettle,' interrupted Alice, 'give the girl something stronger — tea indeed, what would people think? Never let it be said that Alice MacIntosh doesn't put herself out for someone in need. I'll get you something warmer to wear — I've a nice wee shawl upstairs that would look just right on you.' Feeling pleased with herself for her charity, Alice went upstairs and brought back the shawl together with a pair of fluffy sheepskin slippers.

'Put these on your feet — you'll not mind, I hope, if I don't take you ben the room, but I've just had the suite re-covered, and your clothes are a wee bit grubby — I'm keeping it clean for Ne'erday.' Hugh looked at Alice.

'You could put a bit newspaper on the seat, Alice.'

'Don't be daft. The lass doesn't want to go in there. Go and make up the bed in the spare room. She'll need somewhere to sleep,' and lowering her voice so that Beatrice wouldn't hear, 'but don't use the good sheets, I'm saving them for when Aunty Ann comes.' Alice turned to Beatrice.

'Now then, you said you'd brought something? A gift was it? Not that I'm looking for anything, mind,' she added quickly, 'kindness brings its own reward. And as anyone round here will tell you, I've always been ready to help those less fortunate than myself . . . why last year we had a wee boy stay for the whole of Christmas week . . . poor wee thing had lost both his parents in an accident; and then a couple of years ago I made mince pies for the old folks' home — two hundred and forty-seven pies I made, you know. But I don't grudge it, you have to do your bit. Wait till I tell Mrs Lindsay at the shop about this — just like you, she'll say, always ready to help those less fortunate than yourself, and she's right enough. How many other doors did you say you'd been to? And not one of them had the grace to offer you a bed for the night? I hope they're proud of themselves! Wait till they see what I've done — and goodness knows I've little enough to spare! But I don't grudge it!'

And as Alice MacIntosh prattled on and on about all the Good Things she had done over the years, and in how much esteem she was held in the neighbourhood because of it, she didn't notice the gentle 'click' of the door closing. When she turned round Beatrice was gone — all that remained was a little bundle of shawl and slippers.

'No,' said Beatrice to herself as she faced the night once more, 'you're not ready. My gift is not for you.' And once more, Beatrice began to walk.

On and on she walked. Would she ever find the place she was looking for? Three doors she'd knocked on, three sets of people she'd spoken to   but still she knew that none of them was ready yet to receive her gift. Snowflakes began to fall, gently landing on her hair and face, and Beatrice had to swallow very hard to hold back her tears; she didn't want to feel sorry for herself, but she seemed to be the only person on this night who was all alone, and she did so need someone. If she didn't find somewhere to stop soon, she knew that she might lose her precious gift altogether. It seemed to be growing heavier and heavier. Then Beatrice saw a light shining at the end of a short lane, and she decided to try knocking on yet another door. This time, the woman who opened the door looked Beatrice up and down and knew at once what had to be done.

'Oh here you are — we've been expecting you,' she said. 'Come on in out of the cold.'

'I've been to many doors,' said Beatrice. 'I have a gift to offer.'

'Yes, yes — I can see that your time must be near. Now you put your feet up and get warm: we've plenty of time and you can tell us all about yourself later when you're more settled.'

There were three or four people in the house, but none of them seemed to make much of a fuss. They showed her a warm, cheery room where she could sleep, gave her something to eat, and seemed genuinely pleased to be of help. They stayed with her until the time came, and then, when it was all over, the woman who had welcomed her in brought Beatrice a cup of hot, steaming tea. It was the best tea she'd ever tasted. Beatrice looked down at the new baby lying in her arms — surely the most precious gift in all the world. She smiled, snuggled down under the blankets, and went to sleep.

The next morning, after she'd washed and dressed, Beatrice told the kind people in the house that she'd have to leave — she still had things to do.

'I told the others that I had a gift for them, so now I must take my baby to them, and let them share in my happiness.'

'Well in that case, we'll come too — you can't go off on your own again, we'll all go together,' said the kind woman.

They all set off together, back down the road Beatrice had come the night before, and somehow, this time, in the light of day, the street didn't look quite so dismal. The sun was shining brightly, and the snow sparkled on the ground and on the rooftops. The curtains in the windows of the houses were open now, and when the happy little group came to the first door and knocked, Alice MacIntosh opened it at once.

'Well I never!' she exclaimed, looking at Beatrice, and smiling widely at the bundle in her arms. 'A baby! If only I'd known! Come in, come in — Hugh, come on and see who's here: you're not going to believe this! You should have told us, lass.'

'We can't stop,' said Beatrice. 'I wanted you to share in my gift, but there are others to visit, and I must be on my way.'

'Just a minute then — we'll get our coats and come with you: it's not every day we get to see a new baby!'

So Alice and Hugh joined the group and, laughing and singing, they all walked on through the snow to the big house where Douglas and Jennifer Hamilton-Armstrong lived.

When Douglas Hamilton-Armstrong opened the door and saw the sight which greeted him, he called to his wife:

'Jen, my love, remember the little waif who came to our party? Look at the gift she's brought! Half a mo, my dear,' and he stubbed out the fat cigar he'd been smoking, 'can't go breathing smoke in the little one's face, can we? Well, what a surprise! You must come in, all of you.'

'We've someone else to visit,' said Beatrice, 'so we can't stop here, but I had to show you the precious gift which money can't buy.'

'Hang on then,' said Douglas Hamilton-Armstrong, 'I'll get the Porsche out of the garage and we'll go too: this is a celebration!'

'Oh forget the Porsche, darling, let's walk — it's a lovely day!' exclaimed Jennifer, and so two more joined the growing band on their parade through the street.

As before, Gordon and Alexis Campbell were in a frenzy.

'That's the turkey done to a turn — now just the sprouts and potatoes to do. I'm still not certain there'll be enough mince pies, perhaps I ought to whip up another batch before everyone starts arriving — what do you think, Gordon?'

'Mince pies, mince pies, that's all I ever hear about. How should I know if there'll be enough? I'll put out the glasses — sherry, do you think? Or perhaps I should warm up some wine? Oh no, there's the door: don't tell me they've started arriving already!'

Gordon Campbell rushed to the door, while Alexis continued to flutter about around the stove. He was less than pleased when he saw all these apparent strangers standing on his doorstep, and didn't even notice Beatrice and her baby.

'Sorry, can't invite you in . . . we're in a bit of a tizz . . . expecting people for lunch. Don't let me stop you singing though, hold on and I'll get a donation: for the church is it?'

He thought they were carol singers!

Just at that moment, Alexis Campbell spotted the pile of envelopes on the sideboard.

'Gordon — you idiot! You absolute idiot! How could you be so forgetful? The invitations — you forgot to send them! All this food, all these preparations, and now we'll have no guests. No-one is going to come!'

In the midst of all this, Beatrice's baby let out a wail. Gordon Campbell stared in amazement. He looked at the faces before him, and he looked back at his wife. Then he smiled.

'Well, someone's hungry, anyway!' he said. 'No guests, Alexis? We've got guests now! Come on in, we'd better see to this little fellow — can't leave him out here to shout for his dinner!'

So everyone was invited to stay for lunch, and as they sat round the table, eating, drinking, chatting and laughing as though they'd known each other all their lives, no-one noticed Beatrice take her baby and slip quietly away: for her journey wasn't over. There were many people who had a share in this precious gift: for this special baby was for all the world to see, and perhaps if you're listening carefully, there may one day soon come a knock on your door. Will you be ready to answer it?   ∎

CHRISTMAS.

At Christmas we have joy and love but we do not always. Somtimes we just think of presents. We think of Jesus, because he was born on Christmas day. I like to think of Jesus on Christmas day because it is His day. I like giving and sharing presents because it reminds us of the wise men and the shepherds giving the gifts to the baby in the manger, which of course was Jesus. I thought of Jesus at lunch on Christmas day. I like love and joy all year round, so I turned over a new leaf that I would not fight again.

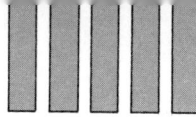

BIBLE STORIES

NOAH'S ARK

The people in the village where this old carpenter lived were wicked — there's no other word for it.

They thieved and spoke foul language and told terrible lies about one another. They cheated each other right and left and they would sell their lovely daughters to the husband who offered most money. And they encouraged their sons to be even bigger twisters than themselves.

And the way they used animals was abominable! They hunted them down and worked them till they were nothing but hide and bone, then they took them to the knacker's yard and sold them for a pound or two. They would put out the eyes of songbirds to make them sing better.

'What's needed in this village,' said the old carpenter to his wife and sons, 'is a thorough *cleansing.*'

The carpenter and his sons began to carry planks of wood, saws, planes and boxes of nails, and hammers, up to the top of the ben. And there they laid the keel of a big boat.

How the villagers laughed when they saw that the old carpenter was building a boat up near the snow-line of the mountain.

'It's come at last,' they cried, falling over themselves with merriment and mockery.

'The old carpenter's gone off his head at last. He's bonkers! He's round the twist. We've seen it coming for a long time. How will the old fool get his boat launched from up there, near the sun?'

The whole village echoed with mockery for days on end.

The villagers laughed even louder when the old carpenter came down to the village post office and sent off telegrams to every species of animal and bird on earth, inviting them to sail with him and his family on the voyage.

They even drove up the mountain in their motor-cars to see how the ship was getting on. They had picnics up there. They pointed at the growing hull, and then fell about laughing. They took thousands of photos.

It was the greatest joke in years.

They took bets with each other as to how long it would be before the old shipwright was carted off to the mental asylum.

Then, from all the airts, the animals began to arrive at the mountain, and climbed up to where the ship was having her final timbers set in place. And you couldn't see the new mast for the birds of every description that fell and furled on the rigging.

'Even the birds and the beasts have come to laugh at old Noah!' cried the villagers.

And at night the villagers would come and try to steal planks and pots of paint. But the snarling of the wild cats and the eagles' screams frightened them off, the scum that they were.

At first the villagers welcomed the rain, for it had been a hot dry summer. But when their thatches began to leak, and their cornfields were beaten flat, and the river began to rise, it was no joke. Night and day the rain fell, incessantly, for weeks on end. The river suddenly overflowed and the dam higher up burst its retaining wall, and the villagers, floating away as best they could on logs of wood and torn-off doors, saw the waters engulf the village and the farms. Those who left last saw that the ben itself was awash half way up. Presently the rising tide lapped at the boat with its cargo of innocents and birds and animals.

'Cast off!' cried Captain Noah from the bridge.

And the world was one huge ocean. And still the rain fell in tumults and torrents. And one after another all the

My Perfect world

My perfect world would be a quiet, Hot sun and have a cool wind blowing cool water to drink. Rosy red apples to pick, lots of trees to play under. Rain every Two days. No war. Every body was happy and warm grass. Long lanes very bendy. Happy squirrels because they did not need to hibernate because there was only one season that was sumer. There are know handy capped people and no colds. It is a happy land with pools all over the place so lots of animals. In the back ~ ground ther is some hills which are beautiful at sunset. And lots of rabbits.

scoundrels and twisters and liars that had infested the village for so long, drowned in the brimming sea of purification.

One morning, Noah the skipper let a dove fly from the ship, through the silver rain. Presently the dove returned with a branch in its beak. Then the sailors knew that the waters were receding, and the world was emerging new and green for good honest folk to live in.

Between the last raincloud and the golden sun lay a beautiful bridge of seven colours: the rainbow. Under it sailed the ship. And through the portholes the sailors could see the earth breaking like a butterfly from its chrysalis, pure and silent and lovely beyond words.

Biblical reference: Genesis chapters 6–8

THE BEAUTIFUL GOWN

When their father and mother adopted an orphan child, Ben and Robert were pleased at first. The child's name was Joe and he was quiet, respectful and undernourished. Because he owned nothing he was given everything new including shoes, shirts, coats, jackets and a brand new case for school; and this was the beginning of the trouble. For Ben and Robert began to think that their parents loved Joe more than they loved them.

One day Robert, who was twelve, said to his brother Ben, who was ten, 'Joe got a new dressing gown today. It's made of silk. And it's got pictures of animals on it.'

Ben, whose own dressing gown was two years old, didn't say anything but looked at his big brother whom he considered his leader.

Robert continued, 'He gets everything new. Mummy and Daddy say that's because he's got nothing. But now he's got everything.'

Ben waited. His brother always had a plan; he was the one who was always making up new games.

At that moment Joe passed them in his shimmering gown coming from the bathroom. It glittered and seemed as if it were alive, with its golden lions and its striped tigers and its huge elephants. Joe said good morning in his polite way but they didn't answer him.

'We must do something,' said Robert, 'we must do something.' His eyes were angry. Ben didn't like it when Robert became angry, and he remained quiet.

'We must have a plan,' said Robert. He didn't say anything more that day but he brooded. Who was this intruder in their house? They had got on so well with their parents but now Joe was the centre of attention. Their mother even told him longer bedtime stories than she told them. She said that no-one had told him stories before and that he was very clever. He listened quietly and absorbed everything. Robert in particular seethed with anger but smiled openly. He thought of Joe as a stranger who wandered about the house in his dressing gown like a king.

One day, Robert said to Ben, 'I know what I'm going to do.'

They were sitting at breakfast one morning when their father, who was a doctor, said, 'I wonder if any of you have seen my cigarette case. I can't seem to find it.' He was very fond of this cigarette case firstly because it was made of silver and secondly because it had been given to him as a present by a grateful patient: in fact he no longer smoked. None of the boys admitted to having seen it. Their father couldn't understand what had happened to it.

They had a maid whose name was Marie; she was eighteen years old and came from France. She was cleaning out the bedrooms when she found the case under Joe's pillow.

'Madam, monsieur,' she said excitedly, 'I have found what monsieur lost.' And she produced the cigarette case and handed it to Dr Fellowes.

'In Joe's room, you say?' he said in a puzzled voice.

'Yes, monsieur, under his peelow.'

Dr Fellowes sent for Joe, who pleaded ignorance.

Finally Dr Fellowes said to him, 'I had thought better of you. Look at what I have done for you and this is the return I get.' For the rest of that day he sat in his study in a sad silence. His wife too turned a cold eye on Joe.

Ben glanced at Robert and realised what had happened. It was Robert who had put the cigarette case in Joe's room.

From that time the doctor and his wife became less friendly to Joe. They sent him to a private school almost as if they wanted to get rid of him. Joe said nothing in his own defence but suffered in silence. He knew, however, who was responsible for his disgrace.

He was in a school different from that of his two foster brothers and was so lonely that he studied very hard, and became the most brilliant student in his class. While he was still in school his foster father died and only his foster mother was left. He often remembered his foster brothers and thought, 'Well, it was natural. It was hard for them not to be envious.' But nevertheless he did feel a slight bitterness.

When their father died and only their mother was left, Robert and Ben, who were now sixteen and fourteen, began to show their real natures, although Robert was the worse of the two and also the leader. When they were home on holiday they would come in late from dances and also ask for large sums of money, and their mother, thinking that she had harmed them by her kindness to Joe, gave them what they wanted. At eighteen and twenty years of age, they began to drink and refused to go to University. They never saw Joe who was still studying as hard as ever; in fact they didn't want to see him.

When their mother died they were left a large sum of money as well as the house, which they sold. They squandered all their money and didn't worry about the future. They bought fast cars and crashed them. They thought their money would last forever. As time passed, their memory of Joe grew dim. They never heard of him and didn't wish to. They lost all their money and were soon very poor, reduced to living in cheap lodgings.

It was a cold winter's night with ice on the street. Ben, now forty, and Robert, thirty-eight, came out of the warm pub. They saw in front of them a jeweller's window which blazed with jewels of all kinds. They stood in front of the window and studied them. Then they looked all around them; there was no-one to be seen but themselves.

They had no money at all; the week's dole had been spent.

Robert looked at Ben and Ben looked back at Robert.

It was a most peculiar thing but the jewels in the window reminded Ben at that moment of the glimmering colours of Joe's dressing gown and it came to him as if in a vision that all that had happened to them had begun with that, and he felt resentful towards his big brother Robert. But Robert didn't seem to feel any guilt at all.

Suddenly, while he was still standing in his dream, he saw Robert kicking the jeweller's window, as if he wished to break in amongst the fiery jewellery. A star appeared on the window but the glass didn't break. At that same moment there was the harsh jangling of an alarm bell and a policeman came running towards them across the ice. They stood there as if transfixed and then began to run. They might have got away if it hadn't been for the slipperiness of the ice, for Robert slipped as he was running and Ben waited for him and before he knew where they were they were handcuffed and in a van.

When they were in the police station, the sergeant said to them, 'You can phone a lawyer if you wish.'

Robert replied gruffly, 'We can't afford a lawyer.'

'In that case,' said the sergeant, 'the state can provide you with one. There is a Mr Agnew who is very good, they say. He spends his time helping poor prisoners.'

All the time they were in the cell the brothers didn't speak to each other, except that Robert once said, 'That was bad luck. If it hadn't been for the ice I would have got away.'

The cell they were in was cold and miserable and they recalled more luxurious days. Suddenly a policeman opened the door of the cell and said, 'Mr Agnew to see you.'

At first they didn't recognise him but he recognised them in spite of their ragged appearance. It hadn't occurred to them that their foster brother Joe would become a lawyer. So the three stood there in that miserable cell till finally Joe said, 'Don't you recognise me?'

It was Ben who recognised him first.

'You're Joe, aren't you?' he said quietly.

Robert raised his head and said in a bitter voice, 'Now I suppose you'll get your own back.'

'My own back?' said Joe. 'What do you mean?'

'You know it was me and Ben who framed you, don't you. All those years ago.'

'Yes,' said Joe, 'but it was my own fault too. It was hard for you, I understand. I've thought a lot about that incident.'

Then in a change of tone he said, 'I believe you were trying to break into a jeweller's shop.'

'Yes,' said Robert, and then suddenly, 'It was just me. Ben had nothing to do with it.'

Joe's face became suddenly radiant.

'I see,' he said. And it was only then that he embraced both of them and it was as if they really were brothers.

Robert stared at him in wonderment.

'You mean,' he said, 'that you are going to help us?'

'Yes,' said Joe, 'why do you think I became a poor man's lawyer? Now sit down and let's talk. I feel responsible for you.'

A prisoner, carrying his shaving gear, walked past, wrapped in a grey blanket.

'You see,' said Joe, 'they don't have nice bright dressing gowns in this place. There is nothing to be envious of here.'

'I understand,' said Robert, and it seemed as if for the first time that he really understood.

Biblical reference: Genesis chapters 37–45

Dear God when I was little I told Fibs I'am sorry.
We thank you for food to eat and things to smell and teachers to teach us about work thank you for freinds to care and to be as happy as can be.
amem

Jacob loved Joseph more than all his other sons and gave him a robe of many colours.

DAVID AND GOLIATH

The two villages at either end of the sea-loch had never got on very well together. Each village boasted that it had a better fishing fleet than the other, and better houses and gardens too.

And 'Oh,' one lot would cry to the other on a still summer night across the water, 'our lassies with the golden hair are bonnier by far than your thin lazy stupid black-haired trollops.'

Sometimes the young men of the two villages would have a punch-up on the day of the cattle-market. Then the ring-leaders would have to appear in court, with their black eyes, and be severely reprimanded by the Sheriff.

The village elders deplored such wild behaviour. 'Get rid of your rage and jealousy on the football field,' they told the young men, over and over.

So after that the villages played football against each other four or five times every year, and sometimes the village of fair-headed people won, and sometimes the village of dark-headed people won, and often it was a draw. Then the twenty-two young men would drink together and laugh and sing till closing time.

One winter, the village of the golden-haired people discovered a new striker, a giant of a young man, as tall and fierce as a Viking, called Goliath. Nothing could stand against the skill and sheer power of Goliath. All the village teams round the loch and along the glen were soundly thrashed, one after the other, by scores such as six-nil, or ten-one, or seven-two, and one even thirteen-two. The hero of every match was the new striker Goliath. He tore defences to shreds and tatters. It was rumoured that Rangers and Liverpool had sent scouts to observe and report on this marvellous young giant of a striker.

And then arrived the date of the first winter match between the two village teams. It was a terrible humiliation for the raven-headed people. They were pulverised. They were cut to pieces. At the final whistle the score was nine-nil.

The defeated eleven were too ashamed even to drink with the victors. As they slunk off home, they could hear from the pub counter the thunderous mocking laughter of Goliath, who had scored seven goals.

People are different

Some are large, some are small,
Some are fat, some are thin,
Some are happy, some are sad,
People are different.

People are black, and some are white,
People are brown, and some are yellow,
People are red, and some are pink,
People are different.

Some are policemen, some are nurses,
Some are firemen, some are maids,
Some are fishermen, some are cooks,
People are different.

People are religious, some are not,
People are voting, some are not,
People are caring, some are not,
People are different.

The return match was due to be played the next Saturday.

There was a boy called David who helped his father on the sheep farm. David was very keen on football — he went to all the matches — but he was only fourteen and played in the juniors.

Arrived the afternoon of the great game. Two bus loads of supporters from the blonde village turned up to cheer on their team, spearheaded by the powerful Goliath. They were certain of victory.

When the home team took the field, it was seen that they had only ten men. Jock McKissop the sweeper hadn't turned up. Everybody knew why; he was so ashamed of the pathetic showing he had made the previous week.

The trainer saw David on the touchline. 'Come on, boy,' he said. 'Get ready. You must play.'

The forlorn faces in the home crowd were not exactly more cheerful when the boy David ran on to the field in his red and white shirt. He was a very small thin boy. The huge Goliath could have blown him away, it seemed, like a dandelion seed.

That Saturday afternoon a new star was born — the equal of Kenny Dalglish or Gordon Strachan or Graeme Souness. Right from the first whistle Goliath the mighty was quenched like a candle-flame. The boy wonder nipped Goliath's every move in the bud. Goliath, baffled by David's superb and subtle craft, time after time, resorted to brute force. It was like trying to stun a trout in the stream, or a blackbird in its bush, with a hammer. If once or twice Goliath gathered the ball, it was swept from his boot in the twinkling of an eye by David and despatched into the enemy penalty area; where no less than five times Bob Grant, rounding a defender, stretched the net with it. How the home crowd cheered! You could have heard their raptures in Ullapool or Oban, each time a goal was scored.

Half way through the second half, Goliath was led off the field limping, like a ham-strung ox.

'That boy,' he snarled, 'kicked me when the referee wasn't watching!' Even his own team-mates knew that that was a lie.

It was the end of Goliath's career. His team was beaten twelve-nil.

The latest news is that Juventus and Real Madrid and Anderlecht are after David in full cry, to sign him. But David is still looking after his father's flocks, and quite content meantime to play for his village team on Saturday afternoons.

They have been unbeaten all season, and are of course top of the league.

Biblical reference: 1 Samuel chapter 17
■

ESTHER

This is the story of a young woman of great loveliness — Esther — whose name is given to one of the books in the Bible. At the time when our story begins, Esther lived in a little village in Persia, now called Iran, in the house of her uncle, a good man called Mordecai. Because her mother and father were dead, Mordecai had brought her up and looked after her; but our story begins not in Mordecai's little village house but in the great palace of the King of the land. The palace of the King Ahasuerus. And at the beginning of the story is a great feast; the King was celebrating. He was happy. Everything in the world was going his way. He ruled a kingdom that stretched from Ethiopia, through Persia as far as India. He was a proud man and had more than anyone on earth could ever desire. And above all he had a Queen whose beauty matched perfectly all his golden riches and all his kingly power. Her name was Vashti.

So great was the feast that he gave for all his princes and nobles and servants that it was to last for seven days and was held in the court of the garden of his palace. In that place everything was of the finest silks and cottons: of white and green and blue. Royal purple curtains were suspended from marble pillars by silver rings. Even the couches were of gold and silver set on red and blue and black and white marble. Nothing was ever more glorious and the guests drank as much of the best wine as they wished from individual goblets of silver and gold.

The King felt glorious and on the last day of the feast, merry with too much wine, he was boasting to the whole company of the great beauty of his wife, Vashti; he said she was the most beautiful woman in his whole kingdom, in any of its one hundred and twenty-seven provinces. He was flushed with drink and pride and to prove his words he sent a chamberlain to fetch Vashti the Queen so that he could exhibit her beauty. And an expectant hush fell on the people at the feast.

Now at that time Vashti was holding a banquet of her own for the women of the royal house. In that country, as in many countries of the east, the women were of great modesty and it was thought to be shameful for a woman to parade herself before the eyes of men. And so when the chamberlain came into the banquet of the women and told Vashti of her husband's demands, everyone was silent waiting, waiting to hear what Vashti would say.

And she said, 'Tell the King, my husband, Ahasuerus, I will not come.'

The chamberlain returned to the King's feast, to where he lay waiting on his golden couch, and nervously he told the King Vashti's words.

At that Ahasuerus threw his golden goblet on the floor; the red wine spilled over the white marble, his eyes burned and without a word he left the feast. His pride was broken in front of all the people and his revenge was terrible. Vashti was never to be allowed to see the King again. But that was only the beginning: so great was the King's anger that he sent out a decree to every province in his Kingdom, in the language of each province, that no woman in his kingdom was to disobey her husband; and even that was not the end of his revenge. He wanted to crush Vashti's spirit and so he sent messengers on mules, camels and dromedaries to every part of the kingdom to find a young woman more beautiful than Vashti that he would take as his new Queen.

And that is how Esther comes into our story. The legend of her loveliness and beauty had spread and she was one of the many young women from all parts, from as far even as India, that were brought to the palace of Ahasuerus so that he could choose his new wife. Ahasuerus had a great eye for beauty. Many lovely women did he gaze upon but when he saw Esther his breath was taken away. She was to be his Queen. He would have no other. And so she was kept in his palace and prepared for her wedding day. No-one from the world outside was allowed to see her or to talk to her.

Before she was taken to the palace, Mordecai, her uncle, had time to say only one thing to Esther. He told her to conceal from everyone, even the King himself, who her family was and that she was a Jew; and wise advice this turned out to be.

But now Mordecai was broken-hearted at losing Esther and spent every day walking up and down before the court of the women's house where she was kept, hoping to hear some word of her, wondering how she was and what had become of her. But Mordecai was a thoughtful man, and a clever man, and one who could bide his time, and so he managed to get himself a good position looking after the official documents of the King's palace. And so at last at the end of one year when the King made Esther his new Queen, Mordecai could, from time to time, talk to her.

Mordecai one day chanced upon documents which showed that two of the King's chamberlains planned to have Ahasuerus killed. Mordecai told this to Esther. She told the King and the King at once had the traitors hanged. A record of this affair was kept in the Palace Book of Chronicles. Mordecai had saved the King's life.

And so it seemed that all was going well for Mordecai and for Esther but not for long, because the King promoted over every prince a man called Haman. Now Haman loved nothing more than himself. The first thing that he did was to issue a decree that every prince, noble and person in the land should bow before him as he passed. And this Mordecai refused to do.

So great was Haman's anger that he determined to destroy not only Mordecai but all his family and all his people, the Jews. He set about this in a very cunning way.

One day when he and Ahasuerus were alone, Haman said to him, 'Oh mighty King, oh Ahasuerus, ruler of one hundred and twenty-seven provinces, oh great one, there are people in your kingdom who do not obey your laws, who do not follow our God.'

The eyes of the King blazed with anger.

'Who are these people, good and faithful Haman? Who are they?'

'The Jews,' said Haman, 'and if it pleases you, oh High Majesty, I shall have these people, to the very last one — man, woman and child — destroyed.'

'Let it be done,' said the King and walked alone into the innermost court of the garden of his palace, a sign of death.

Fear was in the heart of every Jew in the land and Mordecai was in deep despair, wearing filthy sackcloth as a sign of his broken heart. He prayed to his God and an idea came to him.

He sent a message to Esther to tell her of this terrible decree and the danger for all of her people. The message asked Esther to go to the King, to Ahasuerus himself in his innermost chamber and beg him for the lives of her people. Now, no-one dared to go to the King in the innermost

Dear Lord
We thank you for
everything around us
For our friends who
help us get through bad times
And those who love us.
Amen

chamber of his court for to do so without the King's own invitation meant certain execution.

Back to Mordecai, Esther sent the messenger who said, 'Esther asks you to fast and pray for her. She and her maidens too will fast and pray. She will then go to the King in his innermost chamber even if that means death. Her last words to me were, "If I die, I die." She will go.'

Meanwhile the wicked Haman was dancing for joy. He would be rid of the man who would not bow to him, he would be rid of all his family and all the Jews in the land.

To his wife he said, laughing, 'I have built a wooden gallows fifty cubits high and from it Mordecai shall be hanged.' And his wife hugged him. Together they drank a goblet of wine.

'We shall be the people most honoured by the King in the whole kingdom.'

At the end of three days praying to her God, neither eating nor drinking, Esther rose and made herself ready. With great care she prepared herself, her black hair shone with the lustre of ebony. She wore a gown of the purest silk and it was the blue of the sky. Erect and graceful she walked straight past the astonished court guards and into the innermost chamber of the King. Ahasuerus sat on his throne. When he saw Esther before him he was astonished but something in the grace of her walk, in her beauty and her courage, moved his heart and he did an amazing thing. He lifted his pure gold sceptre and pointed it at Esther so that she might touch it. This was a sign that her life would be spared.

'Esther, my dove of beauty, my Queen. What would you have? Ask anything at all even up to half my whole kingdom and it will be yours.'

'Come to my court of women tomorrow,' she said. 'Bring Haman with you and we will all three dine together. Then I will tell you my request.'

'It shall be done,' said the King, and smiled for he was happy to have a wife of such beauty and such courage.

That night the King was uneasy. He could not sleep and to pass the time he read the Palace Book of Chronicles. In it he discovered that Mordecai had never been rewarded for the time that he had saved the King's life.

On the next day he summoned Haman.

'Haman,' he said, 'how would you reward a man who had served the King faithfully and well?'

Haman was beside himself with delight. He thought that the King meant him.

'Great Ahasuerus,' said Haman, wriggling with pleasure, 'I would give him the King's own royal garments to wear. I would put the King's own crown upon his head. I would seat him on the King's own white stallion and I would have all the people watch him ride through the streets in triumph.'

'Good,' said the King, 'I commission you, Haman, to make sure all this happens to the Jew, Mordecai. Tomorrow.'

Haman had to do as the King commanded but on the next evening, the very evening he was to dine with Esther and the King, he banged his fists against the walls of his house and wept. And then the chamberlain came to bring him to the banquet. It was a fine banquet. The proud Haman was unusually quiet even though it was so high an honour to dine with the King and his Queen.

On the second day of the banquet the King said to Esther, 'Now Esther, my Queen, what was the request you wished to make?'

And very quietly, Esther replied, 'Save my life and the life of Mordecai and the lives of my people.'

'What? Who would dare ask for your life or the life of Mordecai, a man I have honoured?' shouted the King.

Esther's eyes flashed. 'That man!' And she pointed to Haman. 'For he wishes all the Jews dead and they are my own people.'

At once the King rose, and strode alone into the innermost court, a sure sign that Haman must die, the sign of death.

And so it was that Mordecai was spared, that the order against the Jews was withdrawn, and the gallows — fifty cubits high — that Haman had built for the purpose of hanging Mordecai, found another victim, the wicked Haman himself.

Biblical reference: The Book of Esther ■

THE PICNIC

My Dear Uncle Nathaniel,
Mum is not allowing me out of the house today. It's a punishment, but I don't regret anything. I'm writing this letter to tell you about it. I also want to ask you something — a sort of favour. Anyhow, this is how it happened.

It was a beautiful morning yesterday here in Bethsaida — I asked Mum if I could go fishing. Well, she agreed and made me a picnic basket with five of these little barley loaves you like. She had just baked them. She put a cooked fish in the basket on each side of them and made me promise to be back by the middle of the afternoon. Well, that's why I'm not allowed out today. You can guess if you like, but you could never guess why I was late. Not in a month of Sabbaths.

Anyhow I took my basket and my fishing rod to that rock you showed me amongst the green grass on the quiet side of the sea of Galilee. You know, just below the hill of the Horns of Hatlin. It was too hot for the fishes I think because I didn't catch anything but suddenly a huge crowd of people, hundreds, thousands, came flocking along the shore like a big herd of sheep.

Have you heard of a man called Jesus? He comes from that wee village Nazareth. Anyhow, the crowd was following him and some of his friends. And they stopped just where I was fishing. Everybody was full of excitement and stories. I heard some people saying that King Herod had a feast and one of the dancers that he really liked asked him a favour: she wanted John the Baptist's head cut off and brought to her on a plate; and the king did it. Have you heard anything about that?

Anyway, this man Jesus spent the whole day telling stories and healing people: crippled and bent people and even one who was mad. As you know I'm still not very tall and I couldn't really see what was going on, and this is the beginning of the really fantastic bit of the story of yesterday.

I was trying to see this Jesus but I was kind of squeezed between two big men and they pushed me out of the way. Suddenly Jesus saw me and he turned and his eyes were burning and he said to these men, 'Make room, let the children come to me, because heaven is made up of people that are like children,' and then they made a space for me and some other kids right beside Jesus and his friends and that's how the next amazing thing happened.

It was really a miracle uncle. Mum and dad don't believe me. They think I'm lying and that's why I'm telling you. You see, two friends of Jesus, a man called Philip, and

> Thank you God for this food we eat.
> Carrots, Potatoes, Peas and Meat.
> All this food you make for us
> We'll eat it up without a fuss.

THank you Lord for the food to eat

Thankyou Lord for the lovely treats

Thankyou Lord for giving us teeth,
to eat the lovely food before us.

Andrew I think the other was, said to Jesus, 'Master, send all these people home. It's hot, we've all had a long day and everyone is starving and there's no food.'

After that everything happened really quickly. I don't know what made me do it but I jumped up and said, 'I've got five loaves and two fishes,' and gave this man Philip my picnic basket.

He laughed when he saw it and was going to hand it back but Jesus took it from him and He actually thanked me. It was amazing. I'm not quite sure what happened next, uncle, but I swear by everything I know that what I say is true. Jesus spoke in a clear, loud voice and divided that whole crowd into about a hundred groups of fifty. He seemed to look up to heaven to bless the loaves and fishes and the next thing I knew was that every single person in that crowd was eating loaves and fishes until we couldn't eat any more, and at the end there were twelve baskets filled up with leftovers. It was brilliant!

Then Jesus told everyone to go home and he sent his followers off in a fishing boat and he went alone up into the hills above the sea, up that valley into the Horns of Hatlin.

Suddenly a great storm blew up. It got dark and of course when I got home Mum was furious because she was worried and I was late and they didn't believe any of this anyway. I think Jesus and his friends are coming to where you are in Capernaum. Try to see him if he comes. How do you think he fed all these people? Write and tell me what you think about this Jesus,if you see him. Mum doesn't like me using the word but I think he's magic and I don't regret anything.

Best wishes,
Your nephew,
John.

P.S. I forgot about the favour. Would you take me fishing again soon and I'll show you exactly where all this happened beside our fishing rock?

Biblical reference: John 6: 1–15

$\mathcal{P}$EOPLE

DAVID LIVINGSTONE

For months our party had struggled through the African jungle, skirmishing with hostile natives, crossing malarial swamps, rushing rivers, looking and hoping to hear some word of this one man. A few days before, we heard yet another rumour and we followed it to this little native village and suddenly, unbelievably, there in flesh and blood he stood before me, in the middle of this village in the jungle — the great man himself. I stumbled forward, held out my hand and said the only words I could think of: 'Dr Livingstone, I presume?' He answered only one word, 'Yes'. 'I thank God that I have been permitted to see you,' said I. 'I am very grateful I am here to welcome you,' he replied.

And that was it. I felt like walking straight up and hugging the old man, but he looked so, well, British, standing there, that one white man in this little African village in the middle of the jungle, miles from any place. So instead of hugging him I took a closer look at this legendary man. He had a grey beard; he looked pale and weary; he wore a bluish little cap with a faded gold band, and a red sleeved waist-length coat. But these words, 'Dr Livingstone, I presume,' were to echo round the whole world, yes, long after the great man was dead. I suppose you could even call it one of the most remarkable meetings in history, Dr Livingstone and me. I'm Henry Stanley, newspaper reporter for the New York Herald. My boss, Gordon Bennett Jnr, our Editor, was looking for one of the biggest newspaper scoops of all time.

For the world was wondering, what the mischief had happened to David Livingstone? He had not been heard of for, yes, for years. He was lost in Africa. So Gordon said to me, 'Stanley, find Livingstone — no cost spared' and I found him after ten months in the jungle, at Ujiji on the 10th of November 1871. Some scoop! He invited me into his native hut and the grand old man insisted that I should take his seat. So I did, and took the chance to ask a thousand questions. This is the remarkable story he told me:

David Livingstone's Story
This is the story David Livingstone told Stanley:
In 1840 I embarked on the steamship from England and after a sea voyage of three months I reached Cape Town in Africa; and that is thirty years ago and for most of these thirty years I've been on this great continent that I love — Africa. Oh, I've been home once or twice, but mainly my life has been Africa. Strange how God takes a hand in a man's life. You'd hardly think a lad who worked in a Scottish mill in the tiny town of Blantyre would spend his life in a vast land like Africa. But clear as a voice in my lug, I knew God wanted me to come here, so I came as a missionary of God's word; but they always blamed in me the urge to explore. And you know, to me a missionary and an explorer are the same thing. You don't need to be a dumpy man in a long coat with a book under your arm. I am a missionary, an explorer and a doctor. You know, I first came to Africa because of the words of a man called Robert Moffat, another Scotsman. It was at a meeting in London. I tell you, he inflamed my imagination. He spoke of the Dark Continent and the smoke of a hundred villages. In my mind's eye I could see the whole parish of all Africa open to the word of God and I was determined to go, I was convinced it was the will of God that I should go, no matter who or what opposed me.

Not of course that it was all opposition — no — God provides in unexpected ways. Aye, I was a lucky man. I stayed when I first came to Africa with that same missionary, Robert Moffat, whose words had inspired me to come, and it was his daughter Mary that I married in 1845. We were wed at her father's missionary station in Kuruman.

She's been dead nine years now, my brave Mary. Yes, nine years.

> Mary lies on Sherpanga brae,
> And keeks fornent the sun.

Yes, Mary is buried in the Africa she loved. It was a hard hard life for a woman but Mary had the courage of a lioness. A long time ago now Mary and myself and the children and a waggon drawn by oxen crossed the Kalahari desert. That was what made me certain that the family and Mary should go to Scotland. Our journey across the desert, you see, was nearly a disaster. As I was telling you, we were

Wouldn't it be nice
If the world was at peace
Treat people like a brother
And be good to one another.

Wouldn't it be nice
If we all had food to eat
For sharing is caring
And the world was at peace.

Wouldn't it be nice
If man didn't destroy the world
Let life continue
For every boy and girl.

Wouldn't it be nice if colour didn't matter
And war was a thing of the past
If people didn't have guns or bombs
And let the world last.

three, and then four. We were near death. Not a word of blame from Mary but oh, when I looked at the tears in her face, when I saw the agony written there! Well, we were almost done. . . . But on the fifth day . . . a miracle! Some bushmen appeared, as if from nowhere, with that most valuable of all needs — water.

But that did it. I knew I couldn't ever submit my wife and family again to such a risk and yet I also knew that I must go on with God's work in Africa, so in April 1852 from Cape Town, my brave Mary and the children left for Scotland. To leave my children without a father, like orphans, was like tearing out my innards. And I missed Mary's sunburnt face, her kind looks. Oh, I loved her when I married her and the longer I lived with her the better I loved her.

But one thing had burned itself into my mind with the force of a branding iron and it was that one thing which made me know I had to stay in Africa.

You see, Mr Stanley, I saw some terrible things, things I can never forget as long as I live. I saw little children chained together to be sold as slaves. Once we passed a woman tied by the neck to a tree, and dead. She had been unable to keep up with the other slaves in a gang. The slave master preferred to murder her in case she recovered after a rest and became someone else's slave. And this happened again and again, again and again. And I thought that this could be my own wife, then my own bairns, so I stayed. And you know, Mr Stanley, if you live among these Africans you remember only that they are fellow men and women. And I was haunted, haunted day and night, by these long lines of slaves.

I determined to oppose this trade, to tell the world about it. I know, Mr Stanley, that even if half the truth were known, this devilish traffic in human flesh would be put down. And, Mr Stanley, you know, God has strange ways. I remember vividly one occasion when we were able to help. It happened like this.

Myself and a small party of Englishmen were on our way to the village of an African friend of mine. Suddenly, round the hill came a long line of men, women and children, manacled together with chains. The black

travelling by a Cape waggon. Day after day passed under a constant sun and there was no sign of water. The oxen were exhausted. Our bushman Shoko searched far and wide but still no water. 'No water, no water,' he would shout, 'all country only, no water.' And then we woke one morning and he had disappeared, so we were left parched and without a guide. The children were whimpering in distress. The less water we had the more thirsty the little rogues became. Two days we had without water, then

slave-drivers were armed with muskets and were blowing tunes on horns as they marched alongside the slaves in triumph. But as soon as they saw our English party, they fled into the jungle never to be seen again. Well, we had to saw through the forked sticks around the necks of the slaves to free them. Two of the women had been shot the day before for trying to escape. Some of the children were five years old. So, you see, I really had to stay here. I had to open up a path into Africa for honest trade instead of this devilish traffic; and a path . . . for Christianity. And I had to let people know of this open sore of the world. Ah, yes, I made a speech about it when I was back visiting England . . . I remember exactly what I said. Oh, I was filled with fire and I said:

'I direct your attention to Africa. I know that in a few years I shall be cut off in that country which is now open. I go back to try to open up a path to Commerce and Christianity.' And then I shouted very loud:

'Do you carry on the work that I have begun! I leave it to you.'

Meantime I returned to Africa inspired with this aim of opening a path for honest trade and Christianity, and oh, I explored.

We made a great journey from Cape Town to Luanda on the west coast and then we crossed right over the continent to the east coast. We covered six thousand miles, most of it on foot, and it took just under four years.

It was hard, crossing rivers, crossing swamps, cutting through deep jungle, and once I was mauled by a lion, Mr Stanley. This arm still troubles me. I laugh when I think about that big fierce cat pouncing on me. I felt like a wee mouse and wondered which part of me it would eat first. Luckily one of the men shot it before it devoured me!

I've had fevers off and on for thirty years now but if the Lord gives me strength I shall not grudge my hunger and toils. Above all, if he permits me to put a stop to the evils of the inland slave trade, I shall bless his name with all my heart. I'm thrawn, you see, Mr Stanley. That's a good Scots word meaning stubborn. I want to find the source of the river Nile so that the world will be forced to sit up and listen to me, so that my mouth will be opened with the power to tell of the enormous evils of the slave trade. I shall do this or perish.

This is where David Livingstone's story ends:
I begged the old man to come with me, home, to rest. But he was as he said, 'thrawn'. And I, Stanley, was the last white man to see David Livingstone alive. He died two years later in 1873 but his body was to take one last long journey. His faithful natives cut out his heart and buried it under a Mulva tree. A monument stands there today. They dried his thin body in the sun, embalmed it with salt and brandy. And in case tribes would know they were carrying a body, they drew up his limbs in order to make him fit into a smaller casket. And they carried the body of David Livingstone fifteen-hundred miles to the sea. It took them nine months walking. From there it was shipped to England.

Many wept at that funeral; on his grave were written his own words against slavery:

> All I can say in my solitude is, may
> heaven's rich blessing come down on
> everyone — American, English or Turk
> — who will help to heal this open
> sore of the world.

And I count it a privilege to have helped a little because that ancient horror of slavery not so long after the death of that great man was, indeed, abolished.

Some scoop! ∎

MARY SLESSOR

My name is Mary, Mary Slessor, Mary Slessor o Calabar they came tae call me, aye Calabar. Ye'll hear mair aboot that in a wee minute.

I wis a Scots lassie, a Scots quine as they'd say in Aiberdeen where I wis born; that's a while syne. It wis on December the 2nd, 1848, so that wisna yesterday. But I didna die in Aiberdeen, na, nor in Dundee, no even in Scotland. Na, na, sixty-seven years later it wis, in Africa, in West Africa, in the tropical bush, aye in Calabar. That wis where it wis all tae end. Except that in a way it disna end at all. It wis just a wee beginnin.

But weel, I'm gettin aheid o masel. I wis aye impulsive. A wild lassie really, in Dundee; aye, when I wis eleven we moved frae Aiberdeen tae Dundee. Ma mither, ma faither, ma brithers and sisters. And in Dundee, dae ye ken whit they cried me? 'Fire, fire, fire! Carrots, carrots, carrots!' That's whit they called me. (It wis because o ma hair.) It wisna whit ye'd call an easy life in Dundee at that time. (I daresay it's no easy noo.) We used tae bide in a single end, the one room just; that wis eight o us, weel, when faither wis in at nicht. And ye'll hear mair aboot faither. He wis a good man, faither, but the very devil wis in him when he wis at the bottle. At a gey early age I had tae ken hoo tae deal wi a drunken man. Often when we were bairns, ma faither, poor mannie, had mither and ma sisters in a rare state o nerves. Late at nicht, intae the hoose he wid stumble, roarin and shoutin, 'Where's ma meat, woman? Dae ye call that burnt offerin a dinner fit for a man? Here's yer supper back!' — and he'd throw the plate, supper an all, into the fire. The children were terrified. He couldna help it I suppose. But when I wis tae meet wi drunken men o a different sort, aye and a different colour as it happened, I kent whit tae dae.

Thae were dark times — and we got used tae one hard visitor tae oor hoose. He took ma faither, and he took four o ma brithers and sisters. Ye'll have guessed his name. . . .

It wis specially hard for mither when Robert died; he wis ma elder brither. Robert wis tae have been the missionary, maybe even tae have gone tae . . . Calabar. At that time ma 'sainted mither' and the rest o us attended the Wishart Church in Dundee, doon at the east end o the

We are all the same.

Dear Father
Some of us are Coloured
some of us are White
But in some way We are all the same.
We may live in different countries towns, cities and regions but We are all the same.
In some countries there's famine and many people have died.
Yesterday an air crew has been killed because their space ship blew up.
We thank you father for friendship and all the love you give
Amen.

Cowgate, just by the Port Gate. That kept us in hert, and always, in the still o the evenin, ma mither wid talk aboot David Livingstone, the mission in Africa, the dark continent. I got tae ken thae distant names — magical, aye and fearsome: the Gold Coast, the Ivory Coast, the Slave Coast, the White Man's Grave. . . .

But maist of all the talk wis of oor Christian mission in Calabar. And whit hurt me maist wis tae hear that the tribes in Calabar pit new-born twins in the jungle tae die. But Calabar, aye, Calabar. That name wis like a flame in ma breist.

Weel, I wis just a lassie workin twelve hoors a day in the Mill wi ma mither. But the flame grew to a fire.

Fire, fire, fire; carrots, carrots, carrots! Fire, carrots, fire, carrots, fire, fire, fire! Aye, ye'll mind that wee rhyme.

I decided tae prepare masel tae be a missionary. Oh, we heard tales o David Livingstone in thae days and had he no been a mill worker like masel? Had he no educated himsel readin while he worked? Weel, so could I, lassie or no. And that's just whit I did, stairted tae educate masel. I got permission and like David Livingstone I got on wi ma readin at the same time as I worked the machine. In fact they pit me in charge o two looms. That name, David Livingstone, pit mair fuel to the fire.

And I started where I wis, richt there in Dundee. I became a mission worker and losh, that wisna easy in Dundee in thae days either. The men were mair interested in their own fecht for better conditions; there wis plenty drunks tae mock oor work, for I used to read the Bible and tell stories aboot Jesus richt there in the street. I mind one day specially, because ye see, in a gey strange-like manner, this work wis God's way tae prepare me for Africa, for Calabar. This wis a kind o apprenticeship. But as I wis sayin, I mind one day specially weel.

On ma way tae the mission, I wis surrounded by a gang, and their leader thocht he could stop me. He wis swingin a muckle lead weight on a string in circles roond his heid, swish, swish, closer and closer, swish, swish towards me until it wis flashin in front o ma face, inches awa, gettin closer. I just stood, fire in ma eyes, blazin, and he dropped it. That wis the carrots and the fire in me; ma

red-heided temper and blue blazin eyes. And ye ken — I got some o thae Dundee toughies tae help in the mission work, wid ye believe it? It wis Jesus gave me the courage.

And when I got tae Africa I wis tae mind on that boy and that lead weight, and years later that wis tae gie me courage when ma very life wis in danger. But ye'll hear aboot that later. Meantime, I battled on at Mr Logie's mission in the slums o Dundee, aye up an daein, but I got mair courage. And at last I applied to the Missions Board in Edinburgh tae see if they wid accept me tae gang tae Africa. Tae Calabar. Folk thocht I wis daft. Nobody expected tae live long in the White Man's Grave. But I wis determined and when I got the reply frae the Missions Board in Edinburgh, I could hardly open the letter. But I tore it open, I read it, and I stairted tae greet like a bairn. They had accepted me.

On August the 5th, 1876, three years efter David Livingstone had died in Africa, I sailed frae Liverpool in England, aboard the steamer 'Ethiopia'. I sailed for Calabar. I wis beginnin the biggest adventure o ma life. Frae the 'sunless rookeries' o the Dundee slums we steamed over the Bay o Biscay and oot o the Atlantic ocean towards thae mysterious places, places stark wi cruelty — the Ivory Coast; places stained with greed — the Gold Coast; places that ran blood-red wi inhumanity — the Slave Coast. Past the Gulf o Guinea we sailed, the hert of tho slave trade, and on tae the malarial mangrove forests and . . . the White Man's Grave.

On September the 11th we sailed oot o the blue waters o the Atlantic intae the mud-coloured estuary o the Cross and Calabar rivers, wi the giant river Niger on oor left, and at last the very scent o Africa wis in ma nostrils. And I kent stories o this land o spices, slaves, gold dust, ivory and palm oil. A place o hunger, fever and death. Parrots flew in flocks from sandbanks and mudbanks, alligators slid intae the murky water. Above me I could see the ruined barracoons where countless black men and women had been penned before they were shipped tae America. A tingle o naked fear came over me. We were aboot tae arrive at Duke Town, fifty miles up river frae the Atlantic. Aye and what wis waiting for me?

Here it wis, a land wi people ruled by witchcraft and secret societies; o skull worship and blood sacrifice; o trials by boiling oil and the poison bean. A land where the death o a chief meant slaves were buried alive and his wives strangled tae keep him company in the next world. Where girls were sent tae farms tae be fattened up for marriage. But aye, it wis the thocht o the twin bairns that widna leave me and I made a vow: 'I shall fecht this . . . it must be stopped . . . I will never gie up.'

So all the way frae Scotland, frae Dundee, I had arrived — I wis twenty-seven at the time — in Calabar at the Mission Station in Duke Town. But it wis aye onward and inward I wanted to gang. I couldna be daein wi some o the smart folk in Duke Town. They were a wee thing refined for me and they didna much approve that I'd climbed every tree in the neighbourhood that wis worth climbin. So I wis wantin tae be up and daein, gangin inwards intae Africa, and along any way that wis what God wis tellin me tae dae. That wis whit he'd pit me here for. And so I wis at last lowsed, I wis free tae gang inland tae the Okoyong tribe.

Noo maist o the white folk thocht I wis clean daft and thocht this wid be the end o me. The Okoyong tribe hadna a very good reputation ye see. For a stairt . . . o yes, mind I wis telling ye aboot the twins? Well the Okoyong were a very religious tribe as well as a savage one. They believed in Great Spirits — in fact they were much mair religious than a lot o folk in Europe. Tae them, the spirit world wis just as real as breid and jam tae us. They couldna be like some white folk I've kent whae switch religion on and off tae suit themsels. So in a way, ye see, we had something in common. We were baith religious. Only their God wis often no as gentle and, as ye'll hear, no as powerful as ma God, and that's somethin they were slowly tae get tae ken.

Oh aye, this business o the twins. Weel, they believed that one twin wis a child o the devil. And since they couldna tell which one it wis, they killed the baith. Aye, they broke their backs, crushed their heids, and left them in jars in the jungle, while their poor demented mither wis banned frae the tribe. Weel, I couldna be daein wi that. But maybe Jean wid be best tae tell you aboot this side o Africa. Ye see, Jean wis ane o thae twins I wis telling ye aboot; she

wis aboot tae be killed and I kidnapped her. But, yes, ye'd be best tae hear aboot that frae Jean hersel. ■

Mary in Calabar: Jean's Story
I was the lucky one. I have often heard the story: Ma Slessor heard that twins had been born to a woman of the Okoyong tribe — that was my brother and me. So Ma made a trip through the jungle and kidnapped both of us because she knew we would surely be killed. But then Ma got very ill with the fever and could not be so watchful and they stole my brother back again. Ma was so ill she was like to die so the mission folk in Duke Town were sending her back on the steamship to her own country, Scotland. And Ma knew that if she left me behind, my people would get me, so she refused to go without me. She said she widna gang withoot me. So it made quite a stir when she stepped off the train in Dundee in Scotland carrying a little white bundle with my face showing. Not many people in Scotland had seen a black face at that time. Ma said I was much admired. But of course not many of our people had seen a white face, especially not a face like Ma's, very pale it was. And oh, when she was angry! She was like a fire; her blue eyes burned, her hair was like a flame, it was as red as carrots. Fire and carrots, she was, and her skin so white. She was small as well, but as she would say to us, 'Guid gear aye gangs in wee buik'.

Oh, but I have seen her stand in front of big chiefs at a big Palaver when they were wild with drink. I have seen her stand like a burning rock and I have seen the chiefs melt like chocolate in the sun. I have even see Ma cuff a man's ear as if he was her little son and still they did not harm her. And our people never forgot how Ma Slessor's medicine cured the illness of Chief Edem.

But once Ma was near to losing her life. It was the time of the big Palaver over the slave man and a young warrior's wife. You see, it was forbidden among the Okoyong tribe for a wife to give a man food if her husband was not at home. They took it as a sign that she was a bad woman. Now it happened that a hungry slave man came and asked the young wife Sonu for food. But Sonu refused because her husband was not there. The slave man threatened her with blows. So to be rid of this fear she gave the slave man food. But some sharp-eyed person saw it and told the Council of the Egbo. They met and found Sonu guilty. Her punishment was to have the boiling oil poured over her naked belly. Ma Slessor heard the drums.

It was a black night. People were gathering. A big circle of torches flamed in the market place. In the centre, a great fire was burning. The girl was staked to the ground. And on the fire the oil was boiling. The men were mad with drink. They wore masks. And then, one man ladled the bubbling oil into a big pot. The girl was terrified for her life, and screamed and screamed. The Chiefs sat in a great circle and waited. And Ma Slessor answered fire with fire. She walked into the circle; she was burning, her eyes were aflame, she was like a volcano. And if she was afraid, nobody knew it.

The masked man with the heavy ladle prowled and edged towards her. Round and round his head he swung the ladle. Nearer and nearer to Ma's head. Suddenly God put into Ma's head the time in Dundee that the boy had swung the lead weight nearer and nearer her face. Only, this time she stood in danger of her life. Beyond the fire the jungle was black; the chanting of the tribe grew quieter; only Ma stood in the firelight with the man swinging madly the ladle towards her face. The fire of her God flashed and blazed in her eyes. In the silence the ladle crashed to the ground. Ma bent, and picked it up and threw it away. The girl and Ma were saved.

And always Ma's family grew. Ma rescued more twins and they became my brothers and sisters. Ma took us with her to Scotland once. Me, Alice, Maggie and Mary. It was funny to be in that land with its cold rain, and cold mist, and streets of stone and houses of stone. So different from when we were in my country and we slept on the grass or in a mud hut. Oh we had everything there — goats and dogs and cows and mosquitoes, and babies, babies everywhere. It was a big family Ma had, and her bairns as she called them helped to take the Book to all the tribes round about.

We set up schools for learning. Ma taught hymns and we used to sing them. And Ma cured people with her medicine, but her best medicine was kindness. She looked after all the people. And Ma walked miles and miles through jungle. She could walk as fast and as far as any man.

Then Ma became sad, very unhappy because she was too weak to walk and take the Book and medicine and God to the people, and so somebody sent Ma a bicycle. It was so funny when she learned to ride it. What a sight, a lady flying along, not walking, on two wheels. To us it was like a miracle.

And then poor Ma got too weak to ride her bicycle. She had too many sicknesses, too many fevers; she was getting old. But still she wanted to go on, always on, so we made a cart and the children used to pull her in the cart.

But it was near the end of Ma's African journey. I was at her bed when she died. She was sixty-seven years old and tired out. The people of the Okoyong and all the tribes from miles and miles came from everywhere to the funeral of 'The Good White Woman who Lived in the Bush' — she who was called 'Mother of all the People', she who was called 'Lady of Fire and Carrots' — but as Ma said, 'it wisna an end at all, mair just a wee stairt'.

Oh! our mother, she who loved us,
She who lost herself in service,
She who lightened all our darkness,
She has left us, and we mourn her
With a lonely, aching sorrow.
May the great good Spirit hear us,
Hear us in our grief and save us,
Compass us with His protection
Till, through suffering and shadow,
We with weary feet have journeyed,
And again our mother greets us
In the Land beyond the sunrise.

GEOFFREY SHAW

The following are stories about Geoffrey Shaw as remembered and told by his friend, the Reverend John Harvey:

Geoffrey Shaw was a friend of mine. Now he is dead, but when he was alive, he and I used to work with children in Glasgow in an area called the Gorbals. The Gorbals was a poor area; for most of the folk who lived there life was hard, and for many of the young people there didn't seem to be much of a future. Heavy drinking and drugs were real problems. Even the surroundings were grey and dismal.

In the summer we used to take some of the kids away to camp with us in the Highlands. These children had never been out of Glasgow, never even been out of the Gorbals, and so they didn't realise what it was like in the Highlands. Rivers, hills, open spaces were new to them, so new that these things even frightened some of them at first. But on the whole they took to life in the open and enjoyed the sizzling meals around the campfire, and the sing-songs at night were great. We even made a record of our songs when we got back to Glasgow — it was called the 'Tayvallich Sing Around'. Geoff loved that record.

One time Geoff took some children to Iona to camp. When they arrived they went for a walk along the village street. Well, you know, in that part of the world everyone always says 'hello' to everyone else as they pass by. So Geoff was walking along, saying 'hello', 'good morning', 'nice day', to just anybody he met. The boys followed him along the road silently, saying nothing, but when they got to the other end of the street, they said to him, 'Geoff, do you know everybody on this island?'

Geoff said, 'No, not at all, it's just that here in the country you say "hello" to people'.

So on the way back after they'd been to the village shop, I can imagine that Geoff was surprised and highly amused to discover that the boys were going up to every single person they met and saying 'hello there', 'how are you doing?', 'fine day!', 'keeping all right them?', and so on.

Geoff was a remarkable person. He was a Christian and he tried to live the way God wants us all to live — the way of Jesus. I'd like to tell you a few wee stories, which I think will give you an idea of what Geoff Shaw was really like, and each story is to do with kids.

The first one, I think, shows you how he wanted to be with kids, all the way. We used to go sometimes to camps near Skye, the island of Skye, and he took boys from Glasgow who had never seen the sea before except perhaps on television. I remember one boy he took with him — he had him there for about three months — and this lad learnt how to sail a fishing boat, an inshore fishing boat with a big motor; he learnt how to sail that boat all the way from our campsite right round the point and up to Skye, and back again. Now this was a very tricky thing for anybody to do, never mind a small boy from the Gorbals in Glasgow. Geoff was very proud of him.

Then, back in Glasgow, a few months later, I remember walking the streets one night with Geoff. Oh, it was two or three o'clock in the morning before we were finished. We were trying to find that same boy, following him round all the places where he was trying to get drugs, because he'd become hooked on what we used to call pep-pills — nasty things that give you a kind of thrill but make you very sick afterwards. In the good times and in the bad times, Geoff was with that boy, doing his best for him. He was *with* the kids and *for* them. Totally *for* them.

Geoff was a minister, and one day he baptised one of our children. On the day of the service he came along, dressed as a minister, and he climbed into the pulpit to preach the sermon before the baptism and he stood up to preach, and then suddenly, to everyone's surprise, Geoff sat down again. You couldn't see him because he'd sat right down and buried his head in his hands. Well, everybody was very worried: we thought maybe he'd been taken ill. So I went up to see what was wrong and found him crying. Yes, grown-ups can cry, and he was crying, because all the previous night he'd been searching for one of his boys, a boy of fifteen perhaps, who had got himself into awful difficulties. It was discovered that he had finally thrown himself into the river Clyde, and drowned. Geoff had tried to find him to stop him, and failed. So he was terribly upset. Yes, he was *for* them, even in their darkest days.

Mind you, sometimes he had quite a fight on his hands. The first camp I ever went to with Geoff was on Iona. It was a beautiful period of the year, I remember, a clear sky, the sea glistening, a really hot sun. We were under canvas in a few tents. Geoff and the boys had been there for a few days. However, when I arrived at the campsite, I was surprised. Everything was quiet. There was no sound of laughter, high jinks, and carry-ons, and no sign even of the boys kicking footballs about. Very strange.

Indeed, the boys were inside the tent on this beautiful hot summer's day, wearing their city clothes, which in those days included ties around their necks, playing cards and smoking cigarettes. All this was in the middle of the afternoon.

Outside was Geoff. He was rattling around in an obvious fury, dressed in shorts and sannies, really angry because the boys would not take off their ties and city clothes, or come out and play football with him, or climb hills or sail boats or even go swimming. They thought the best thing to do on holiday was to play cards.

Well, he was furious. He wouldn't speak to them for days. But then, later on during that camp, he persuaded some of them (and I was with them) to go to one of the services in the Abbey of Iona. Some weren't too keen to go. They had never been in a church. They thought it would be boring, full of stern and serious grown-ups who would tell them to be quiet all the time.

Well, I'll never forget the look of surprise on their faces. I think you have to call it real surprise on the face of one of these boys in particular. He was astonished: when he went into the church, the first thing that happened was (after people had said 'hello', which was surprise enough) that some young people with guitars stood up in the middle of the Abbey and sang 'We Shall Overcome'. And the boys could not help but join in. Guitars in the church was something they could all enjoy.

Geoff Shaw introduced young Glasgow people to lots of things, and maybe the greatest thing about him was that he was available to young people at any hour of day or night if they were in need. He would turn no-one away. ■

The World

Rain,
And sun,
Happiness,
And fun,
That's what the world has,
For everyone.

Sleet,
And snow,
Frost that makes,
Our fingers glow,
And wind that will freeze the world,
In one big blow.

Loving,
And caring,
Kindness,
And sharing,
Tying the world closer,
Together with string.

I WAS A PRISONER

This is the true story of a man who spent many years in prison. This is the story he told:

My name is Bill McGibbon. I spent the best years of my childhood and my adolescence from fifteen onwards making a complete and utter mess of my life with drink and with drugs. One thing led to another. I needed money to feed these habits; to buy the drink and to get the drugs. And to get the money I turned to crime, stole from the company I was working for, and then finally went to prison. I was discontented and unhappy so I became more and more violent. The charges against me got bigger: at first breach of the peace or drunk and disorderly, but later police assault, violently resisting arrest. I became more and more aggressive towards my family over the years and the charges steadily mounted. Soon I came to be known on the streets as Big Wullie or Gibby. Not the Bill McGibbon I am today. I was supposed to be a husband and the father of two children. I was neither: I was the biggest wean in the house. It was as if my wife had two daughters and this big adult male to look after — and I was the most trouble.

As the days and the weeks and the months and the years rolled on, I started going to prison more often and for longer sentences. And then I ended up in jail for attempted murder; the big one! I almost took another man's life, a man who had a wife and two kids just like myself. In prison I found myself with a lot of time to think about things.

When I was in prison before this sentence, I put on a brave front and blamed everyone else for my problems — particularly the police and the warders. I wasn't at all down-hearted. But this time I began to realise one thing — I realised that I had lost my freedom. That was the punishment for me, for really I had enjoyed life: I had worked hard, played hard. But now here I was in prison: now I was *told* when I could go to the toilet, I was *told* when I could get a wash and shower, I was *told* when I could go to work, I was even *told* what I could work at — despite any skills I had — and I was *told* what kind of clothes I could wear, and *told* when I was entitled to a change of clothing. I was even *told* what and when to eat and what to eat it with: plastic knives and forks. Instead of this, I could have been sitting at home eating with real knives and forks and being with my family. Yes, what I lost more than anything else was my freedom. I started to feel remorse, to feel sorry for the wife and the kids and to vow I would never commit a crime again when I got out. But when you get out you forget all these promises very quickly.

After twelve years of drinking, fighting, ruining a promising football career, losing a good job with my company, I had found myself in prison for this latest sentence — for attempted murder. And I was determined that the lads who had grassed on me — who'd told the police — would suffer when I got out. I was at that time, a very hard-hearted, very bitter man, dependent on booze and drugs to keep me going.

Then one day the prison officer opened the door of my cell to talk to me. It was a Sunday afternoon. He said, 'Bible class?'

I said, 'Whit's that?'

And he said, 'Bible class — yes or no?'

Well, I thought to myself, let's get out of the Peter for a while — that was our name for the prison cell — and go along and listen.

So I went along and listened and there were some guys at the class with a couple of guitars and they sung Country and Western Gospel music I had never heard before. I quite enjoyed that. But when the man started to preach about Jesus and God and things like that, well I just went to sleep same as all the other guys. Generally when we went along to Church service on Sunday mornings, we used it as a chance to pass notes to each other, to pass tobacco and different things. But the Bible class wasn't the same, because these guys seemed to enjoy what they were doing. They were very sincere; they were always like that, and what is more, they were happy. It wasn't the old ideas I had about Church at all — black suits, white shirts, pews, that sort of thing.

I went along the following week and listened and I went back again the week after that, and so it went on. I went along and listened and listened. And one week the man said to us, 'You've really made a mess of your lives, haven't you?' He was very direct.

And I said in reply, 'Well, that's a bit unfair, you've got a captive audience here. But I suppose you have been very kind to us up till now'.

But the man said that all we really had to do was to ask God, the Creator of the world, to forgive our sins, whatever our sins might be; those things which we had done wrong in our lives. We could have those things completely wiped out of our lives, just by asking God, the Creator of the world, to forgive us.

Well, I thought to myself, that seems a bit easy. I went back to my cell. That Sunday I was reading a book. About three-quarters of the way through it I came across this bit that said: 'Forgive me, God; against thee only have I done this evil and sinned in thy sight that thou might be justified and thou judge'. And I thought to myself, well, that's true. It wasn't really the fault of the jury that I ended up here, or

the judge, or even the prison officers: I was here because of what I did wrong. And if what the man said in Bible class is true, then all I have to do is to ask God to forgive me. And if he forgives me, then I can go back into society, take my rightful place, become a father, become a husband, get back to work, look after my wife and kids, get back my mother's love and my father's, get back my self-respect, my self-esteem, my self-worth; I can get back into society and enjoy life and stop being a fool.

When I read those lines in that book, I just got down on my knees in that prison cell and I said, 'Right Jimmy, whoever you are, come into my life. If you are going to do all these marvellous things, I'll have none of these past convictions to answer to any more and the police'll no hassle me when I get out of this place, and I'll no want to go with the same guys any more and get into the same trouble again, because really now I have had enough! I think it's about time that I faced up to the responsibilities I have as a father and a husband — as a human being — and stop messing everyone about. I want just to go home and have my kids say, "Hi, Dad, nice to see you home," and mean it'.

So I asked this God, this Jesus, into my life. That was January the 7th, 1972. I felt wonderful the next morning. I felt really at peace with myself and my mind and in my heart. Next day, I said to the guys I was working with in the mailbag section, 'I'm fed up with fairy stories; I believe what the man at the Bible class said on Sunday. I have decided to become a Christian'.

Well, I got out of prison at last, and of course my family were scared — they thought that maybe this wouldn't last long. But as time went by, we proved a lot to each other. My daughters both love me very much. I always get a wee kiss even though I'm forty-one and they're married now. But the important thing for us all is that now I am an ex-convict with Christ.

In the early days, just after I came out of prison, my wife was still unsure of me because of the problems I had caused her in the past. She just didn't trust me at first. One time she even followed me down to the wee Mission Hall I went to in Kilmarnock Road — the Bethany Hall. She thought I was getting all dressed up to go out on a Saturday night just as usual, to get drunk. But the strange thing was, I never did seem to come back drunk. This puzzled her. So she followed me all the way to the Mission Hall only to discover me sitting there in all innocence. You know, I used to be very good at dodging around Glasgow in the bad old days, but I never even noticed her behind me. She wanted to see just exactly what I was up to and finding me at the Mission set her mind at ease a wee bit. She still didn't trust me fully, but she decided to go along with me to the meetings; we would go as a family, to help me get back on my feet again.

But one day came the real test. I was back in Glasgow at Bible College. I was with my wife when two guys attacked me in the street. They wanted Big Gibby's reputation, you see. She was terrified about what I might do to these guys because I'd been a real hard man in my time. But I just said

to them, 'Now look, this is silly. You and I both know that I don't have a reputation now. I've got a new life-style and I'm not going to change that by fighting you guys. So let's just sit down and talk this thing through'. Now, for my wife to see that! For her to see me sit down and say to these two Glasgow hard men from Priesthill that God loved them as much as he loved me, well that was for her the turning point. And that was six years after I had come out of prison; for six years I had been a Christian. That night my wife said to me, 'Now I trust you'. Because she'd never really seen me put to the test in the streets until that day. It was the streets where I had done most damage. That was the clincher for her, you know. She had been through the last six years and things were good and nothing had really gone wrong, but she had never felt that she had seen anything that would really challenge me, that would really make me break and put me back in the spot where I would react with violence. But she'd seen just that in the street with the two men from Priesthill. Six years: oh, it was a long time for her really. It wasn't something like, 'Oh, he's become a Christian, great, fantastic, everything's alright and rosy in the garden and we'll never have any more bother'. No, my wife had to wait a long time to see the change in me because I had to work hard at it myself first. God is good in that respect: he gives you an ideal and he gives you his text book and you go along with it the best you can.

Well, I *have* found a certain peace and enjoyment after all, because here we are, thirteen years later; I have my wife and the rest of my family. I've even got a wee baby boy about twenty months old. So although I didn't see my first two kids growing up because I was drunk on and off for about twelve years, now I change nappies and put him to bed; him and I play a lot together during the day, and we like to go walks on a Sunday morning. We say prayers before we go to bed and have lots of fun. I missed out on all of that before. As the father that I was, and the husband that I was, I gave my family a terrible time.

Looking back, I can see the difference in me now and I have to thank this God, I really must be honest. I wouldn't change any of this new life. I love everything about it: I run a wee football team over here where I live, I'm doing refereeing now, officially, and I've got a marvellous job. I am doing all right.

I've even worked in a borstal since I came out of prison: I worked in a girls' List D school in Dundee for four years, and I never told any lies to get the job. It was because I wanted to work with kids who'd made the same mistakes as I had.

In that List D school in Dundee, I learnt that all these kids were there because their parents didn't or couldn't care enough, so they were outwith parental control. They were in there for truancy from school; they were in there for shoplifting among other things. But they were shoplifting because they wanted to eat. And I had grown up to that way of life in the east end of Glasgow, so I understand.

Anyway, I enjoyed that job and my employers sent me to University in Dundee and I studied social work there. I learnt a lot about myself through going to University. I've got no O' levels or Highers to speak of, by the way.

Then, many years later, the Band of Hope were looking for a new full-time secretary to deal with preventative education in schools, more specifically in Primary and Secondary schools, Boys' Brigades, Girls' Brigades, Junior Brigades, Scouts and Life Boys. These groups are representative of the young people in Scotland, part of the increasing force of youth in Britain as a whole. The message is simple: the Band of Hope want to say to the young people today, 'There are dangerous consequences if you mess about with your lives, if you use or misuse drugs for instance, and we are here to tell you about them!'

Well, the Band of Hope offered me the job. I had been in residential social work for ten years until that point and I felt that it was time to move out of the cure game and into the educational game where I have remained ever since — working for prevention.

So you see, if there are folk who say that there's no hope for an ex-convict, I've got news for them. There is hope. I hope that you understand that and I hope that all the kids out there do too. ∎

Freedom

If I was locked in prison I would miss swimming and living with my family and going to shops and supermarket.
I would miss sitting with my family having tea, I would miss my friend's and pet rabbit Sooty.
I would miss getting out to play. I would maybe miss school.

THE ANGEL

This is the story of a boy called Angel, as told in the words of James Morton, the Dean of the Cathedral of St John the Divine in New York City:

I want to tell a story that would be very interesting to Scottish young people because it has to do with stonecutters and you have got a lot of stone in Scotland. At the turn of the century we used to have many many people from Scotland who came to New York to cut stone and to help build the great buildings of this city. There were about 30 000 Scottish and English stonecutters in the New York area around the turn of the century. The Cathedral which is the Anglican Cathedral in New York was started in 1892, and there were many many Scottish and English stonecutters employed.

The building went along until the First World War then it stopped, and it started again in 1925 and went on until the bombing of Pearl Harbour, which was at the beginning of the American involvement in the Second World War in 1941. Meanwhile the Cathedral was growing each year — literally being built. But in 1941, with the Second World War, the building stopped and it stopped for forty years. It didn't start again until 1979.

The problem was that in those forty years of stillness for the Cathedral all of the stonecutters had grown old. Many of them had even died. And so, when we were getting ready to start building again, we looked around for some stonecutters and there weren't any — not one. Well, perhaps a couple, but they were old men in their eighties. There was however one man by the name of Three-Finger George. But he was eighty-three years old, and although he had worked on the Cathedral back in the twenties, he was much too old to work now. And so there we were, wanting to build again, with stone, but not having any stonecutters.

So what we decided to do was to go to the only place we could find stonecutters — Great Britain. At that time, Liverpool Cathedral had just been finished. And so I came over from America and went and talked to the master builder, and the place was full of stonecutters. But he said, 'We in England have had a hard time and we've had to train

people ourselves to be stonecutters, which is the old way'.

And I said, 'Well, we don't have any stonecutters, so could you come to America and train some of our people?'

And he said, 'Yes, I'll come.'

So he came over to New York City and started training young men and young women living around the cathedral to be stonecutters.

Well, around our neighbourhood most of the young people came from the south; from Puerto Rico and from the Caribbean, and most of them are black and coloured young people. And that was terrific because there happened to be a very high unemployment rate particularly among black and coloured people in New York, and so training them to be stonecutters would not only train a whole new generation of stonecutters but would also give employment to people who were not employed.

The first five people who worked with us were really remarkable. There was one young man whose name was José, and José was seventeen years old and he was Puerto Rican — born in Puerto Rico — and he had not finished school. He couldn't read very well, but he was extremely, extremely agile and he turned out to be the fastest stonecutter we had. He just picked up the trade immediately.

And we were looking for more people and José said, 'I've got a cousin and his name is Angel.' He pronounced it 'An-hell' because that's the way Puerto Rican people pronounce Angel.

He said, 'Angel is not so smart. He never really has gone to school. In fact some people say he's a bit slow — but he's very honest and I think he'd be a good person to sweep.'

And we said, 'OK, we need someone to sweep up the stoneyard.' There were lots of stone chips and lots of stone dust. And so Angel came onto the team. Angel was indeed very careful and very loyal and very methodical and he swept beautifully.

Now one day the master mason, who came from Wells Cathedral in England, a man by the name of Alan Bird, was watching Angel, and he said, 'I think Angel could operate the crane that lifts the stones.'

All you have to do in that job is push a button, because it's an electric crane; but you have to be very precise about putting stone upon stone. The stones can weigh as much as ten tons — those are the biggest ones that come out of the earth. Huge stone boulders that are then cut into smaller pieces by the great saws.

And so Angel operated the great crane, and when he put one stone upon another the master mason noticed that Angel could get one stone on top of the other with about one sixty-fourth of an inch accuracy. In other words, he was operating this immense crane with tremendous agility and accuracy. The master mason started wondering. He remembered that this young man had been advertised as being rather slow and only able to sweep — and he did sweep well. But now here he was doing this very tricky job of stacking stones.

LUCK

Aren't we lucky to have
All we need
Eyes, ears, nose
Tongue and teeth.

Others aren't so lucky as we.
Some are blind and cannot see
Some are deaf and cannot hear
They aren't as lucky as you or me.

'He's smarter than I thought,' the master mason said to himself.

But of course the most skilled job was the job of actually cutting the stone — working with the mallet and chisels; that's what Angel's cousin José did.

As a matter of fact, we didn't think that Angel could ever be a stonecutter because he seemed rather slow. But the master mason noticed that during his lunch hour, Angel was off in a corner with a mallet, cutting stone. Just practising. And so he went up to him one day and said, 'Listen, Angel, I see you are cutting stone in your lunch hour. Would you like to try out to be a stonecutter?'

And Angel said, 'Yah'. Angel didn't talk very much, he just said, 'Yah'.

And so Angel became an apprentice stonecutter. And after six months it became clear that in Angel we had one of the smartest stonecutters we've ever had. Angel indeed was not someone who could read well, in fact he couldn't read at all, but he had a regularity of rhythm, and an accuracy, and a steadfastness in his style of cutting which is exactly what makes the very best stonecutters.

In building a great cathedral you need all kinds of gifts. Some people have got to be able to read very well and some people have got to be able to do very tricky work and think very fast, but most of the people who build a cathedral have got to be dependable and accurate and steadfast. And that is what Angel is.

Now I suppose that people would say Angel might be retarded, that Angel might be mentally slow, but words like that don't mean anything to me, because I look upon Angel and I see the work that he does and it's the very finest stonecutting that we could possibly have. And I've been told now, after we've been at this project for six years, that over the years and over the centuries, when every building was made of stone and there were as many stonecutters then as there are bricklayers today, that people who might seem slow and dull, and might even be called handicapped by some people, were in fact the very finest crafts-people.

■

SAINTS

ST MARGARET

The story of St Margaret of Scotland began long ago in the distant land of Hungary. She was a bubbling, happy child and the people called her their little pearl, because her name, Margaret, meant pearl.

Hungary had just become a Christian country and everywhere the sound of bells calling people to prayer soared high into the blue sky, higher even than the skylarks. The monks' chanting rang round the white-stoned monasteries and all the land rejoiced. What a wonderful place it was for a young princess to grow up.

As soon as she could read, Margaret learnt all about the great men and women who had followed Jesus and had become saints. She longed to have a life full of adventure like theirs when she grew up.

At the age of eleven, Margaret went to England and, as the years passed, she became more beautiful and wise. She was fair like her Saxon people. Her hair was long and braided into a rope of solid gold which, when loosened, fell in soft waves like a field of blowing corn; her cheeks were pink and rosy and when she laughed her eyes filled with mirth.

In 1066, when Margaret was twenty, disaster struck England. The French invaded and Margaret's family had to flee for their lives. They set sail for Hungary, but no sooner were they on their way than the sea grew dark and wild. The seagulls flew to the safety of land as a huge storm arose. Mighty waves crashed down on them and their ships looked like toy boats on the high sea. The family cowered below decks in fear, wondering if they would ever reach the safety of land again. Three long days passed in this way until the storm gradually lost its anger.

Margaret climbed onto the deck, her legs weary from the ordeal. The sunlight was blinding after days in the dark cabin. She peered at the swooping gulls. There, ahead of the boat, was land.

Now the King of Scotland at that time was Malcolm Canmore. He was a warrior of fearsome reputation who had slain many men in battle with his axe. His name — Canmore — meant 'Big Head,' and it was true, he had an enormous head stuck on his shoulders with a wild mass of hair and a black beard. His hands were big and rough like leather and his enemies were filled with terror at the sight of him.

One day, the King was at his favourite sport of hunting when a messenger galloped up at great speed. Panting for breath he hailed the King: 'Strange ships have been sighted in the Forth, Sire!'

Malcolm frowned darkly with suspicion. He rallied his men and set off with the thunder of hooves and their banners unfurled behind them.

There off the coast of Fife were the ships. Spreading out, the King's men drew their swords in readiness.

'In the name of Malcolm, King of the Scots, who goes there, friend or foe?' shouted the messenger. For a while nothing happened, then Margaret's brother appeared. The others followed; they were still weak and held onto each other tightly at the sight of the fierce Scots.

'I am the Saxon, Edgar Atheling, true heir to the English throne. This is my family. We are fleeing from William of France and seek your kind protection.'

The warrior king didn't care whether they lived or died but there was a lot of cunning in that great lowering head of his. William of France was his enemy too and he realised he could keep this family in Scotland as a double threat to the invader.

'Bring the wretches ashore,' he shouted, and he signalled to his men to put down their swords.

Malcolm had not bargained for the effect Margaret would have on him for when he saw her he was speechless. She was tired and hungry; her fine silk dress was soaked with sea salt and her cheeks were pale, but she was still beautiful. Her hair was gold, her smile full of courage. It seemed to him as if she had come from heaven. He wanted to marry her. Of that he was certain.

What a choice faced Margaret! Her greatest wish was to go to Hungary and become a nun. Suddenly here she was in this poor war-scarred country with a brutish King who wanted to marry her.

She prayed with all her heart that God might show her the right thing to do. Days and nights passed until one morning she woke at dawn after sleeping very little. Of course! That was it. She must do God's duty in a way she

Lord

Give us the kindness to listen,
To people who especially need our help.
Give us the patience to sort out their difficulties,
And make the world understand other people's difficulties.

Amen

could never have imagined, by becoming Queen of Scotland; after all, she had been washed up in the Firth of Forth as if by God's will. Sometimes it's not too difficult to find out God's will; it may be staring you in the face all the time but you just haven't noticed. So, with bravery and certainty that this was the right choice, she accepted Malcolm's hand in marriage.

Everyone rejoiced that Margaret was Queen. When she travelled through the countryside people thronged to see her.

One day as she passed on her way she saw people with fair hair like her own pulling a heavy cart. A man was beating them with a stick. Margaret's heart filled with horror and tears rose to her eyes. Why were they being treated like beasts? Her courtiers told her they were slaves. Saxons like herself captured in a raid on England.

Margaret hid her sorrow. In great secrecy she got her most trusted courtiers to fetch treasures from every church in the land. She sent spies to find out how many slaves there were. She was determined to free them whatever the danger, and Malcolm, she said, must never find out.

In the dead of night, when the moon sailed high in the heavens, a silent figure entered the palace and came to Margaret's door. Inside on her table was an enormous pile of gold coins to pay for the release of the slaves. The two made their plans in haste, but heavy footsteps approached. Margaret gasped. It was too late. In charged Malcolm, staring in amazement.

'I'm giving away this money to free the Saxon slaves,' said Margaret, who was very frightened but stared up defiantly. The warrior King was filled with rage and threw the coins to the ground.

'I'm King of this country,' he roared. 'I give the commands!'

Margaret prayed deeply for strength to deal with the King's rage.

'Solomon was the greatest King who ever lived, in war and peace. He showed justice and mercy to his people and earned their deep admiration,' she replied.

Malcolm glowered at her. Secretly he was quite taken with the idea of being like the great King Solomon, but he burst out of the room kicking the door as he went.

Malcolm was confused. He had always thought himself a good King, fighting battles, keeping the English at bay. Of course he had slain thousands of people, but what was wrong with that? That was what a King was meant to do. And now this wife of his was telling him how to run *his* country — to show mercy of all things! What was he to do?

Never a day passed without Margaret performing some act of kindness to the people around her. One morning, not long after the sun was up, she slipped out of the palace disguised as a fisherwife. As she walked along the road she met a young woman who was very distressed. Her baby was sick and she had no money to feed it. Margaret took the baby in her arms and comforted it. It was the tiniest baby, wrapped in rags. She handed the small bundle back to its mother and wished them farewell. The young women returned home. She sat by the hearth where a roaring fire should have been but there were only ashes, and she looked at the cauldron where hot broth should be steaming but

there was none; only scraps for the mice to eat. She was in despair. Then, as she laid her baby down, three gold coins fell out of the baby's ragged clothes. At once she knew that she had met the great Queen Margaret and wept with tears of joy.

King Malcolm loved his wife more dearly than any man could! Sometimes he could be seen watching the Queen as she took the little orphans onto her lap to feed them. Once, so moved was he when she knelt to wash the feet of a beggar, that he fell to his knees to join her. He began to wonder if Margaret was perhaps some kind of saint. And wouldn't it be difficult for him, Malcolm 'Bighead', to live with a saint?

Well, for many years Malcolm and Margaret did live happily together until one day a wicked servant slipped a thought into the King's head. He told the King that Margaret crept away every night to a secret meeting place. Malcolm was filled with jealousy. He could not bear the idea that she might be meeting another lover. The King decided to keep a close watch on his Queen and sure enough, that very night Margaret stole from the palace and down through the Glen. The ancient trees heaved and sighed in the wind and the old owl turned its head and blinked at Margaret as she hurried past. But the owl was not the only one watching her. Malcolm, his heart heavy with dread, was silently following her through the gloom: he could just see her pale figure moving through the shadows. On and deeper into the glen they went until the dark wood almost swallowed them. Margaret stopped. The King stopped. He watched in disbelief as she slipped like a ghost through a curtain of ivy shimmering in the moonlight and vanished.

Malcolm crept closer, hardly breathing. He could hear her voice raised. She was talking to someone!

His heart thumped. He could bear it no longer. In fury he raised his sword, slashed his way through the ivy and burst into a cave, his sword ready to deal death. He froze. It was as if some huge hand had blocked his way.

The cave was hushed. Only the light of a candle flickered on the glistening walls. And there in the corner, all alone, was Margaret, kneeling deep in prayer. She was with her God.

A Grace

Thank you oh God,
For all your loving care.
For food, clothes and shelter
For all the World to share.
Amen.

68

Malcolm's raised sword clattered to the ground. Tears of shame filling his eyes. He had almost killed his own beloved wife. How could she forgive him?

Margaret looked up with gentle startled eyes. She had no bitterness in her heart. She forgave him and the two were united once more in joy. Malcolm grew to love everything she did, and although he couldn't read himself he would look at Margaret's gospel books in wonder, as if by touching them he might magically receive some of her goodness. When she was away on journeys he used to send for goldsmiths to have her books covered in gold and precious stones to make her happy when she came home.

But Malcolm never ceased to be a warrior King and was once more at war with the English. He was about to set off for battle with their eldest son, Edmund. Something told Margaret that she would never see them again. She begged Malcolm to stay but he felt it was his duty as the King of Scotland to go.

By now Margaret was becoming weak and weary. She was helped each day to a small window high in Edinburgh Castle to look for the return of the army. She prayed constantly. She was lying in bed, not far from death, when her son Edgar came to her. Before he spoke he could read death in her face. He bore the terrible news that Malcolm was dead. Their eldest son, Edmund, was killed in battle by his side. Edgar, looking at his sick mother, so near to death, could not bear to tell her. He lied that all was well.

A tear rolled down Margaret's face; she looked up at Edgar. It was plain she knew the truth; her prediction had come true. Heartbroken, she prayed for the last time in the tiny chapel in Edinburgh Castle, which to this very day bears her name, and a great sense of peace came to her. Her fingers loosened their hold on the little cross she always carried and her spirit left her to join the spirit of the husband that she knew God had chosen for her in such a strange and wonderful way. ∎

ST MUNGO

'Miracles?' said the old man, his face crinkling in a smile, his eyes twinkling. 'Is it miracles you want?'

I felt the hot flush come to my face, for the old man was teasing me in front of the others, and sure enough they laughed. But the old man's voice had such kindness in it that I didn't mind. I didn't mind at all. For Mungo was talking to me, the youngest boy in the room.

The fire crackled and smoked, threw its warmth and light round the hut. And Mungo too shed a warmth and light on all of us.

They said he was a saint, and I could believe it. He had two names, and I suppose in a way he was like two different people. Mungo was what we called him in the community. It was the name he'd been given as a boy, and it meant 'dear friend'. But visitors who came to see him, folk from outside, asked for Bishop Kentigern, as that was his other name.

When he was up there in front of us — grand in his robes, leading the mass, with that look in his eyes as if he was talking to God Himself — that was Kentigern. But when he moved among us, talked to us, even joked with us, he was Mungo.

Like tonight. Gathered here in the long hut, the day's work done, bread broken, devotions complete, we sat in that flickering firelight, content just to listen to him speak. He asked us if the boys had any questions for him. And I piped up about miracles, about all the fabulous stories of things he had done.

'Miracles!' he said again, looking straight at me. 'Well now. There's miracles and miracles.' And again the others laughed.

'All right,' he said. 'I'll show you a miracle!'

One or two folk laughed again, but most of them were quiet, expectant.

'And there's nothing insubstantial about this miracle,' said Mungo. 'It's solid. It's a miracle made of iron!'

He lifted something from beside his chair and placed it in his lap. It was wrapped in pure white cloth. Slowly he opened out the cloth to reveal a little bell, which he held up and showed to me.

'There!' he said. 'I brought it here all the way from Rome. And if that's not miraculous. I don't know what is! For I was not a young man when I made the journey. And what with landslides to go round, and skirmishes with brigands, and a storm at sea when we made the crossing, it's a wonder to me that I'm here talking to you at all!'

My mind was on fire as the old man spoke, for I'd heard tales about that journey — how a party of robbers had attacked the little group of travellers, and how Mungo had stood his ground and faced them down, put the fear of God in them with his quiet strength.

'The Lord was with us,' he said. 'We carried His blessing and protection as sure as I carried this precious gift.'

And at that he rang the bell, let us hear its pure clear tone. Then he wrapped the bell once more in its white cloth.

'Miracles,' he said again, smiling at me. 'I could tell you about the bird. And the tree. And the fish.'

I nodded, eager to hear.

'Well,' he said, 'when I was not much older than you, a strange thing happened to me. I lived in a little community not unlike this one, and my master was called Serf. Now there's a thing for you to think on! A master whose name means servant! Anyway, Serf had a wonderful way with animals and birds. I believe there was not a beast he could not have eating out of his hand. And one of his favourite creatures was a little redbreast he had tamed and kept as a pet. Now, I have to say that I too was a favourite of the master, and he gave me the task of looking after this little bird and feeding it with grain. But there were two or three other boys — a year or two older than me — who were jealous of me for the small kindnesses the master showed me.'

At this I felt uncomfortable, for I had known jealousy in myself, had felt it eat at me.

'Of course,' said Mungo, as if he could read me, 'we have all experienced jealousy at some time. The important thing is not to give in to it. Is that not so?'

I nodded again.

'Unfortunately,' he said, 'these boys could not conquer their jealousy. And since they could not take it out on me, they took it out on the bird. They caught it and they beat it with sticks.'

The old man's face looked grim and sad at the memory.

'When I found it,' he said, 'I wept, for it was already cold and all the life was gone from it. But I held it in my hands, as if to warm it. I breathed a silent prayer over it. And I had the strangest of feelings. A great stillness came on me. It seemed to me that my own life-breath was entering into the bird. And I felt the tiniest flicker, a pulse in that little body, and a wind ruffled its feathers. It stirred. And it breathed. And its heart beat. It was alive!'

The old man was speaking quietly now, his eyes shining in the firelight. And everyone else was quiet, straining to hear every word.

'In a few days the bird was chirping and flying around, as healthy as ever.'

He shook his head, amazed at the memory.

'Mind you,' he went on, 'it didn't stop those daft boys. For they tried to make more mischief for me. You see, there was another task that Serf had entrusted to me. And that was the keeping of the sacred flame. The flame burned constantly in the chapel, and my job was to tend it and make sure it didn't go out. Well, these boys had gone in when no-one was there and doused the flame. (I found this out later when one of them confessed to me!) And of course I felt terrible. I had failed. I had let the fire go out. There were ashes in my heart.

'I wandered outside not knowing what to do. And again I felt that stillness come over me. I felt myself drawn to the old hazel tree. It seemed that the tree was burning with a strange unearthly fire. And somehow I knew that the fire would not harm me. For the tree burned and was not consumed. So I broke off a branch and went with it to the chapel. And you know, those boys were laughing at me. For they could not see the fire! To them the tree was just an ordinary tree, and they wondered what madness had taken hold of me!

'Well, madness or not, I knew what I had to do. I held the branch to the bowl where the sacred flame had burned. And I breathed a prayer, just as I had with the bird. And as I prayed, I felt the life-breath flow from me and feed the living fire in the hazel branch and kindle the dead flame. And I gave thanks and went back outside. And the branch no longer burned in my hand. And the tree was no longer ablaze.'

The old man looked at me and smiled.

'Well then,' he said, 'have you had your fill of miracles?'

My Prayer.

Dear God
          Thank-you for eyes for us to see,
And Thank-you for ears for us to hear with,
And Thank-you for arms and legs to act,
And Thank-you for a brain to think,
And the brain to make-up this prayer.
                              Amen

'Yes,' I said. 'I mean no.'

One or two folk laughed again at my confusion. But by now I was completely happed in the old man's warmth, and I didn't blush at all.

'I *did* say I would tell you the story of the fish as well,' he said, 'didn't I?'

I nodded. He went on.

'Now this is a different kind of story altogether. But no less marvellous for all that. It concerns a lady, a gold ring and a salmon.'

There was a murmur among the older men, a chuckle.

'I was much older when this happened,' said Mungo. 'Much longer in the tooth! And God had blessed me with common sense which folk called *wisdom*, and they would come to me for all sorts of advice. So, one day this lady came to me in some distress. She had lost her ring, you see. And while that's not the kind of thing that would normally concern me, this lady was none other than the wife of the king! And she and her husband had showed me great kindness, so of course I wanted to help. But the whole affair was a little delicate.'

Again there was a chuckle from the men. Mungo acknowledged it with a smile, and continued.

'What had happened was this. The ring had been given to her by her husband, the king. But in a foolish moment she had given it away to a young man, her favourite at court. The king had found out about this and become jealous, demanding that she show him the ring. In a panic, she said she had mislaid it, then she went to the young man and asked for it back. Imagine how she felt when he said he had lost it! So the lady came to me.

'I asked her to give me time to consider, and I went to my cell, to pray for guidance. And as I kneeled in prayer, I entered once more into that stillness. And I saw in the eye of my mind an image, like something in a dream. And the image was this — a beautiful shining fish, a salmon, with the gold ring in its mouth.'

As the old man spoke, I could almost see the fish, swimming in clear water.

'Somehow,' said Mungo, 'I knew once again what had to be done. I told the lady to bring me a salmon from the river. I remember she looked at me with some bewilderment! But she sent one of her servants to the river, to carry out my instructions. The man hurried back with his catch — one of the finest fish I had ever seen. I cut it open, and there in its belly was the lady's gold ring!

'She couldn't believe it of course. And she couldn't thank me enough. She left with tears of gratitude in her eyes, praising the Lord and talking of miracles!'

The old man looked at me again, with that twinkle.

'There now!' he said. 'Do you believe all these stories I'm telling you?'

'Yes!' I said. 'Of course!'

'Of course!' he repeated, smiling. 'And in years to come you will often think of these stories, and ponder over their meaning. For you know, our Lord performed many miracles, but he also spoke in parables. And a thing when it happens can have one meaning. Then it is told in a story and becomes a legend, and it comes to mean something more.

'So when you think of these tales I have told you, maybe you will think about the ringing of a bell, and what that might mean to those who hear it. Or you may think about the breath of life and the flight of the spirit, or the hazel of knowledge and the salmon of wisdom. And you may ask yourself about a ring, and the fact that it has no beginning and no end.

'But for now, you stay with your sense of wonder at the simplest things in God's creation. A bell rings. A fish swims. A bird flies. A tree grows. There's miracles for you!'

■

ST MAGNUS

There was a time many, many years ago when everyone lived in houses without electric light. Men fought their wars with swords and spears while the women were often left to dig the land and grow the corn.

And it was to an island called Orkney which lies to the north of the north coast of Scotland that fierce men came from over the sea to steal the people's precious silver, to take their food and to murder. These invaders were called Vikings and they carried with them large swords that could kill you in a flash.

To burn, kill and steal was their purpose; they did it so many times that eventually the people of Orkney gave up trying to defend themselves and let the Vikings rule.

What they loved more than anything else, these greedy men, was to lie in wait by a lonely shore-line for rich merchant ships so they could steal all their gold and silver. It didn't matter if they got killed because they believed that they went to their own special heaven called Valhalla where dead warriors gathered to feast on plenty of food, to sing and dance and stay young for ever.

At that time the Viking king ruled all of Norway and many other countries like Iceland, Scotland and some islands. But these countries were not enough for this man who loved to conquer new lands. So he plotted to invade another kingdom belonging to the Celts. This was Wales. For this expedition the king needed more ships; so he commanded his men to build them and also summoned captains and oarsmen and skippers from as far away as Iceland, Skye and Orkney to fight for him. When all was ready he and his men set sail.

Now the king chose two men from Orkney to come with him as his second-in-command. These young men were cousins. They were Earl Hakon Paulson and Earl Magnus Erlendson. They were both brave and strong and were soon to prove themselves two of the very best, but — as we shall see — in very different ways.

The Viking fleet sailed all the way down from the North of Scotland past the English coast and on towards Wales, a long journey for those times when there were no engines on ships but only sail or oar. Everywhere that they went more ships joined them, because in Ireland also the rulers had to show loyalty to the fierce Norwegian king.

They proceeded south until they came to the Welsh coast, and it was there that, in a narrow channel, they met the enemy fleet of the Welsh all decked out in red sails and commanded by two men who were both earls and both called Hugh: Hugh the Earl of Chester and Hugh the Earl of Shrewsbury.

Both fleets were silent as they surveyed their enemy; Norwegians, Danes, Icelanders and Orkneymen rowed their boats nearer to the Welshmen who were, by reputation, every bit as fierce and brave as they. Archers stood at the ready; the whirr of their arrows as they flew through the air mingled with the splash of the oars.

And then there was the sound of a horn and of Welshmen chanting above the cries of the gulls. This was their war-song which, when sung, stirred the blood in their veins, making them ready and brave enough to do battle. The Viking warriors were not afraid and said mockingly:

'The channel is narrow, Welshmen, there's no room for two ships to pass!'

But the Welsh replied:

'Turn round then. Go back to your sheep and wolves in the North!' And they laughed at the enemy as they shot their first arrows into the air. A Norse oarsman fell down dead on the wet planks of his boat.

The din of battle was deafening: axes and swords clattered on decks — great thumps and bumps were heard as boats collided, cracking masts and timbers. There was the awful, pitiful cries of men in pain as arms and legs were hacked and maimed by sword and axe. Some boats caught fire; bodies encircled in flames fell lifeless into the water.

It was some time before anyone in the Viking fleet noticed that something extraordinary was happening: there in the king's ship amongst all of the terrible killing was a young man dressed in a white linen shirt sitting in the bows. He was holding a scroll and was reading from it. His lips moved silently as his fingers marked the place from where he read the psalms: if you had been standing close by you might have heard the comforting words, 'though I walk in death's dark vale I shall fear no evil . . .'

Whatever it was it astounded the Norwegian king

when he noticed it and he pointed to the young man.

'Who is that coward there?' he yelled. 'How dare anyone in *my* ship not fight.' But his voice was not heard above the cries and shouts and clashes of sword and iron.

The king looked again at the man with the scroll. And he couldn't believe his eyes. It was his trusted Earl Magnus. There he was, out in the open, reading. 'Reading!' the king was struck dumb, 'while all around are fighting tooth and nail!' The king shook his head. 'And he dares do this after I've honoured him by appointing him cup-bearer?' The king couldn't get over the fact that his chosen one was a coward.

The battle continued ferociously, and the sky grew black with arrows. Icelandic warriors met their watery graves while Welsh farmers with swords in their hands sank to the bottom of the sea.

Enemies drew closer and could see the faces of each other quite plainly against the mid-day sunlight. Keenly the Viking king cast an expert eye at his enemy — Hugh the Proud, the tall Welsh earl.

They both paused for a few moments and there, through the silence, came the calm voice of Magnus reading the words of the Lord Jesus. This could not be the act of a coward, for Magnus had placed himself in one of the most dangerous parts of the ship; already three quivering Welsh arrows had lodged beside his very head.

No, this was a different kind of courage — and a courage not known before by the warlike Vikings. Magnus was not hiding behind a mast but was out there in the open available for anyone to shoot him if they so desired.

It was a terrible day for the Welsh: one of their leaders was killed by an arrow shot by the King of Norway himself, and when the Welsh saw him fall they let out a great cry of despair.

But the King of Norway shouted with joy and commanded Magnus to pour wine to celebrate, but Magnus was still reading psalms.

'There's a coward in every battle,' said many of the Vikings.

Ignoring their scorn Magnus folded up his scroll carefully; it was growing too dark to read.

'Victory!' they all shouted. 'Victory!' The Vikings drank and sang and prepared for their long journey back home.

Now, when they returned the king appointed the cousins, Hakon and Magnus, to rule Orkney together. It was not easy, for Hakon loved war and Magnus hated it. Being a jealous and greedy man, Hakon wanted the island for himself. So he plotted to kill Magnus. He waited until the right time came, and seized his chance by suggesting to his cousin that they meet at Easter-time, on an island called Egilsay, to seal their friendship by signing a treaty.

When Magnus heard of the plan he was pleased; he had no reason to suspect his cousin of foul-play. He prepared for the occasion by summoning his most peace-loving men and obeyed his cousin's demand that neither of them were to take more than two ships with them to Egilsay.

While Magnus was preparing to set sail, Hakon was assembling not two shipfuls of men, but eight. Magnus arrived first at Egilsay, and when he saw his cousin approaching with his eight ships, he knew that Hakon had betrayed him and was coming to murder him.

That night Magnus stayed quietly on the island. Knowing his fate, he went into a church and prayed. His men offered to guard him against Hakon but Magnus said, 'I won't put your lives in danger; our peace is to do God's will.' Magnus's love for his cousin was so strong that he wanted to make sure that Hakon would not suffer from guilt if Hakon killed him. So he made an offer saying, 'God knows that I think more of your soul than of my own life; it were better that you should do as I shall offer you than that you should take my life.'

Magnus then offered to be blinded and thrown into a dark dungeon for the rest of his life.

Although Earl Hakon agreed to this offer, his followers did not. They were appalled at the idea of torturing Magnus in this horrible way and said, 'One of you will we kill now, and from this day you shall not both rule the lands of the Orkneys.'

Hakon said that it should be Magnus who should meet his death and he called for his cook Lifolf, to do the foul deed. But when Lifolf knew what he had to do he started to sob uncontrollably.

Magnus tried to calm him down. 'Don't weep, Lifolf!' he entreated, 'you're not killing me because you want to; you're being forced into it, so there's no blame.'

As he said these words, he took off his tunic and gave it to Lifolf. And so, after a short prayer for himself, his friends and enemies, Magnus lay down on the ground and prepared himself for death with joy, saying to his executioner:

'My head mustn't be chopped off; I am an earl and not a thief so let the blow be on my forehead instead.'

He then offered himself up peacefully to his Lord Jesus. A single stroke of the axe killed him outright and his spirit went to heaven.

Today if you go to Kirkwall in Orkney you can see the cathedral built in honour of this brave man. There it stands containing Magnus's bones which were uncovered again this century, nearly a thousand years after his death. And to this day the skull bears the dent where Lifolf's axe put an end to Magnus's life.

The great cathedral and the story of St Magnus remind us that the world can be won not by war but through quietness and peace. ∎

ST COLUMBA

This is the story of St Columba as told by Lord George MacLeod of Fuinary, the founder of the Iona Community:

Columba was a man from very early times. He belonged to the sixth century and that is a very long time ago indeed. We know that Columba was brought up in Ireland where his father owned a large estate. And this was where Columba lived. To tell you the truth, Columba was no angel in those days. For instance, he wanted to get hold of a book, a sort of pamphlet about the Church, but it did not belong to him — it belonged to another boy, called Finnian. At first Columba asked for the book, but Finnian refused. Angered by this, Columba persuaded his father to go to war against Finnian and his people. Several hundreds were killed just because he did not get the book. It is no wonder that I say Columba was no angel.

Columba was at that time a priest. He had already built a church and founded a monastery in his native land. But after the war over the book, he found that everyone at the monastery was against him. They said, 'We don't want you here with us at all'. And so he left Ireland and came to Scotland. He sailed from Ireland with twelve men who became his disciples. After a long journey they settled down on the island of Iona.

The island of Iona is a very interesting place. It existed exactly where it is today long before the island of Mull had been created. Long before the first fish appeared in the sea, the little island of Iona took its place in the world. Yes, it was an extraordinary island that Columba landed on.

When Columba arrived, the Picts and the Scots who lived on the land were at war. The Scots asked Columba to join them on their side, but he had learnt his lesson about the horrors of war back in Ireland. Columba had changed, seeing the death and destruction that had been caused by that foolish war in Ireland. He vowed to be a peace-bringer for Jesus. So he refused to take any sides. Instead he decided to do something about *stopping* the war. With two or three followers called 'Peregrini', meaning they walked barefoot, Columba travelled on foot and in little boats called coracles as far as Inverness, where the chief of the Picts — King Brude was his name — lived with his people.

When he got to Inverness, Columba found the dwelling where King Brude lived, and knocked loudly on the huge bolted doors. But nobody came to open them. The Picts were warlike people and very suspicious of strangers. But Columba did not give up. He prayed to God that the doors might somehow open, and believe it or not — they did! Columba bravely walked in to face King Brude. The King was astonished. So much so that he stood and listened to Columba as he spoke. And Columba told the warrior king that true strength is the strength *not* to kill, not to wound, not to hurt, but to face life with peace and the love of Jesus. And from that time onwards, there was hardly any trouble between the Picts and the Scots.

Columba became a changed man when he refused to fight. He remembered that Jesus said, 'Love your enemy — do good to them that do spitefully use you'. This is called *pacifism*. And this is what we in the Iona Community believe in. We understand what Jesus said as being a heart-felt plea that we should love people who are in difficulties, love people who are bad, who are criminals, who are sad or who are foolish. Love them and you will change people as we ourselves are changed when people are kind to us, even when we have made mistakes and done wrong things. The people who love us matter more to us; these are the people who really change us for the better, much more than those who seek to punish us.

Let me give you an example. For many years we in the Iona Community have organised a Borstal Camp for young people, twenty at once, who come time and time again. Only two people look after the boys and yet, throughout the years, not one of them has run away. I think that is because we showed our care for them and gave them the idea that they are worthy of trust.

(Nearly 1400 years after the death of Columba, we in the Iona Community went to the island on a special visit in order to be able to get together and talk about what we are going to do about wars in this day and age. In the last world war, believe it or not, it was the *Christian* United States of America who decided to drop the first Nuclear Bomb. And in only one day, at a place in Japan called Hiroshima, that bomb killed 170 000 people. No-one can say that it is right to kill men, women and children, and in such high numbers, for any reason at all. Like Columba with the Picts and the Scots, we in the community decided that we are for non-violence. All kinds of wars are wrong. A man in America once said: 'We must either have non-violence or non-existence'.)

Now, let me tell you how our Iona Community came about.

In 1938 I was the Minister of Govan. There was great unemployment at that time. And the thing the men were most afraid of was losing their skills. So I said to some of the unemployed boys, 'Would you like to keep your skills going by restoring an old mill, called Fingleton Mill, that's

broken down? I can't give you money but I can give you a decent dinner. And when you've finished it, you can have the whole place. You can bring your children out of town at weekends and also in the summer time when there is no school, because so many of them have never seen the country'.

So they agreed: we got the place going and succeeded in rebuilding it.

Now I used to go to Iona for the summer because my sister Ellen loved the place. I was on the island with a man from Govan and he said to me, 'Why don't you rebuild the ruined parts of the Abbey?' I said, 'Don't be daft'. But then my sister said to me one day, 'Have you ever thought of rebuilding the Abbey?'

A Perfect world

In my pefect world people would be loving and caring. Everybody liked every body and people had no enemys. Russia and america would not have nuclear wepons. There were no such things as starwars. People would not be too greedy or too nasty. It rained every other day all round the world to make all the crops grow. Flowers would grow In every garden. All babies were born well and not ill. All the country's would be friends. And every one would have a Job. Every one went on hoiladay to Spain, France or Italy, IN MY Perfect world.

I said, 'Don't talk nonsense. I'm very happy in Govan. What do I know about rebuilding Abbeys?' I'll soon put a stop to this, I thought to myself. I'll write to the trustees of the Abbey and they are bound to say no to such a ridiculous suggestion.

So I wrote to them and they wrote back and said, 'What a *wonderful* idea.' So I was still stuck with it. But they went on to say to me, 'By the way, if you are going to rebuild the Abbey, you'll find the money won't you?' So I thought, 'Right. For my next excuse I'll ask people to give me money and they'll refuse and I'll say, well, we can't get the money and we'll stay in Govan'.

So I went to the richest man I knew and he wrote back and said that obviously I needed my head looking at. Who on earth could start rebuilding an Abbey on an island. Ha! The second richest man I knew then hasn't replied even yet — and that was all those years ago.

Then I wrote to James Lithgow. He had the shipyard in Govan. It was only five hundred yards from the door of the shipyard to the church.

I didn't know him very well because at that time I was a pacifist and he was boat-building battleships! So naturally I thought, 'He will certainly fail me, and then I'll be able to say I can't get the money and I'll get out of the whole thing'. But he surprised me by saying: 'Come and stay the night with my family as our guest'. I'd never been asked that before and I went and spent the night with them. He said, 'I've got a small yacht and my wife and I sometimes sail up the west coast and land on Iona. I once asked my wife, why doesn't the Church rebuild this place? And now here is a letter from you. If I give you £5000 will you give up pacifism?' 'Not on your life,' I said. And he said, 'Well, I'll give you the £5000 anyway'. So there was nothing for it but to get started.

So in 1938 I took some workers and some divinity students out to put up huts as living quarters.

While we were there a gentleman staying at the Argyll Hotel wrote a letter to *The Scotsman* newspaper saying: 'Who are these people ruining the peace and beauty of Iona, putting up huts beside the Abbey and putting out their washing on a Sunday?'

> **A Wish For The World**
>
> If I had a wish for the world
> I don't know what it would be
> Because there's so many things that a wish for the world
> That a wish for the world could be.
>
> There's famine in Africa and the people need grain
> And crashes in Jumbo Jet planes.
> Mexico's had earthquakes and landslides
> Britain's had far too much rain.
>
> There is sadness in the world
> Unhappiness, guilt and shame
> I think I'd wish for the world
> To be peaceful and happy again.

That made me angry because by now I was keen to get on with the job. However, a fortnight later we got a letter from a lady I didn't know and she wrote and said, 'I was furious about that letter to *The Scotsman*. Why shouldn't you leave your washing out on Sundays? After all, isn't cleanliness next to godliness?' And I turned the page of her letter and there was a cheque for £10 000; that's about £80 000 in today's money. 'This is most extraordinary,' I thought. So in 1939 we arrived in Iona with four carpenters, four masons and eight young divinity students to work as labourers for these craftsmen. We hadn't been there a fortnight when the Second World War began. We read in *The Scotsman* newspaper that all timber had to be turned over to the government for the purposes of war. So now there was no wood for building the Abbey.

Just then a ship coming from Canada struck so fierce a storm that it had to jettison its cargo, which oddly enough was timber. And that timber floated a hundred miles across the sea and landed on the coast of Mull opposite Iona, a very small distance away. And all the timber was exactly the right length. This deeply moved me and I said, 'I've suddenly realised that God wants this Abbey. We can do what we like but the dear Lord wants it'. From that moment on I was on the side of rebuilding the Abbey. And it now holds worship for people of every denomination.

That's nearly fifty years ago but at the last count, only two years ago, we had two thousand people in the youth camp! It was overflowing with young people.

These are the stories that Lord George MacLeod told about Columba and about rebuilding the Abbey. Now when he told these stories he was in his ninetieth year.

And now a beautiful new centre is to be built on Iona. It is to be called the MacLeod Centre after Lord MacLeod himself; so the work that Columba did all those years ago, and that Lord MacLeod started, is still going on in Iona.

It will continue into the future as well because the Iona Community is training young people to be sort of twentieth century missionaries who, like Columba's monks of old, will go out amongst the people, feeding the poor, clothing them, helping them and taking to them the ancient story of the life and love of Jesus.

Even now, two young girls not long out of school are training to be these new kinds of followers, or 'peregrines', as they are called; named after the barefoot wandering followers of Columba. Of course, they do not go barefoot nowadays. In fact if you met Lynn Brady and Liz Spence, you would think they were just like any other young girls not long out of school.

Lynn left school without O-Grades; she worked in a shop and then in a factory. Life was hard and drab.

But then she began to take what Jesus said seriously: she believed that she mattered. Slowly she learnt to look after other people; children who found life difficult. She took children who had never seen the outside of a city to see the country, the seaside, to places like the island of Arran. When the time came to leave the island, the children stood on the pier and wept because they had discovered so much. They wanted to stay. Now she loves working with all kinds of children.

Liz, her friend, discovered on the beautiful isle of Iona that religion included singing and dancing and laughing and clowning. She has learnt to be a clown; she likes to get young people to make plays and she wants to make a play about the beginning of the world. Maybe you could make a play about the creation of the world yourselves. And maybe, like Lynn and Liz, when you grow older you could find ways of making the people in the world laugh and dance and sing, and enjoy and help one another. Why not?

PRAYERS

Thank you for the mince we get.
Thank you for the vegetables that we love.
Thank you for the clothes that keep us warm.

Thankyou Lord for for food to eat

Thankyou Lord

Thankyou Lord for rain and sun

Thankyou Lord

Thankyou Lord for all the flowers

Thankyou Lord

Thankyou Lord for all the world

Thankyou Lord

And thankyou Lord for Jesus

Amen

About the world

Dear God

We thank you for the homes we live in and the food we eat. We thank you for the sunshine and the joy and happiness in the world.

We thank you for the birds, trees and flowers, and the rain, and the moon and stars. The grassy banks are lovely. Amen.

Thank you lord for the food on this table
Thank you for our parents and our school
Thank you for our life.
Help us go the way we are taght.
Forgive our sins and help us.
Let us live the life we should
Help us settle quarles with our friends.
Amen

Let us Pray

Dear Lord,
Thankyou for my loving parents, my brothers and my dog. I don't know what I would do without them. I thankyou for my friends. I also thankyou for the things that are not so important.

Amen

Grace
Thank you O Lord for food that we eat and for our dinner lady to prepare it.
Amen.

In My Perfect World.

I think a perfect world would be when every body was nice to eachother and shared everything. There would be no children dressed in rags and no illnesses that killed people. And also the country side would be full of animals hoping about and lovely bright flowers. In all countries their would be a little sunshine and a little rain so there crops will grow and everyone will have food to eat. There would be no selfish people who never shared and were all mean and grumpy. There would not be any fighting and there would be no war about people wanting other countries for themselves. That is selfishness which we dont have

... **In My Perfect World.**